RICH AND FAMOUS

The Further Adventures of George Stable

James Lincoln Collier

VOLO
HYPERION
NEW YORK

For Gwil

First published by Four Winds Press, a Division of Scholastic Magazine, Inc. © 1975. Reprinted by permission of the author.

First Volo Edition 2001

1 3 5 7 9 10 8 6 4 2

The text for this book is set in 13-point Deepdene.

ISBN 0-7868-1519-1
Library of Congress Catalog Card Data on file.

Visit www.volobooks.com

CHAPTER ONE

ELL, WHAT ARE you going to do, George?" Stanky said.

"Commit suicide, probably," I said. We were lying around Stanky's room messing the place up with banana slushes we had made in his blender.

"Good thinking," Stanky said.

"You think I'm kidding," I said. I slurped at my banana slush. "Why do you have to go to music camp this summer?"

"Because I want to," Stanky said. "Besides, what difference does it make? You aren't going to be around."

"Maybe I will be," I said.

"What time are you supposed to meet Woody?"

"At three o'clock," I said. "He says this guy is the biggest guy in the record business in New York. He says to be there *punto,* baby." Woody Woodward was always saying stuff like baby and groovy and being places *punto,* which is Spanish for being on time, I guess, although I'm not too sure, because I got a D in Spanish.

"I don't know why you're so worried about it. You keep saying that nothing ever comes from these big deals that Woody has. What about that television show you were supposed to be on? What about that movie you were supposed to be in?"

"I was supposed to be in it for a minute," I said.

"Well, anyway," Stanky said.

"Yes, but this one might work out. I have a feeling."

"Come on, George," Stanky said. "You had a feeling about that movie, too."

I put my banana slush down on the floor beside Stanky's guest bed where I would be sure to kick it over if I forgot and got up suddenly, and lay down on my back. I was feeling pretty gloomy.

"Well, I didn't have the *same* feeling about that movie. I just have a feeling this one might happen. And there I'll be shoved off upstate watching Cousin Sinclair be perfect for four weeks."

"You'll just have to explain it to your father."

"Stanky, give it up, will you? How can I explain it to Pop? I'm not supposed to *know* I'm going to get shoved off all summer watching Sinclair be perfect."

"Did you tell your Pop that Woody has this hot new record deal going?"

"Sure I told him. He just said what he always says, 'Don't get your hopes up, Georgie. These things of Woodward's never work out.'"

We didn't say anything. I felt around for my banana slush without looking.

"You're going to knock that over," Stanky said.

"Where is it?" I said.

"A little closer to the bed. Watch it."

I got hold of the banana slush and had a good noisy suck at it. The Stankys are rich. Well, not exactly rich, but they have plenty of money and they always have straws and things around.

"I'm getting bored with this conversation," Stanky said. "Let's play Ping-Pong."

"I'm getting bored with being beaten in Ping-Pong," I said. "Anyway, I have to go home and get changed so I'll get there *punto.*"

I walked home through Washington Square. It was May. The leaves on the trees were unfolding, the squirrels were running around like mad, the N.Y.U. students were out there without any shirts on, playing Frisbee, and the junkies were dozing on the benches. You can always tell when spring comes in Greenwich Village because the drug addicts come out of hibernation or wherever they spend the winter and take up half the benches in the park.

But I was too worried about my problem to pay attention to spring. The truth was that Pop didn't want me to make a record and get rich and famous and retire at twenty-five. Oh, he let me go to the auditions Woody got me, and he pretended to take it seriously, but that was just because he didn't believe that anything would ever come of any of the means for getting rich and famous Woody was always coming up with. If he'd thought anything was likely to come of them, he'd have blown up. It was his belief that anybody who got into the music business was bound to drop out of school and die of an overdose of drugs about six weeks later. Oh, maybe I'm exaggerating. I don't know what Pop really would have done if any of Woody's means for getting rich and famous came true. But having me sing on a record wasn't going to turn him on, that was for sure.

I took a shower, put on my brush denims and my coolest-looking shirt, which wasn't too cool because Pop won't buy me anything too cool, and took the subway up to Camelot Records. It was in the Camelot Building, a huge thing about eighty stories high on Sixth Avenue near Rockefeller Center. They had a pretty snazzy office—you know, glass tables and gold record plaques on the walls and small trees growing around here and there. But being around the music business I'd gotten used to places like that and when I told the receptionist my name I acted cool and nonchalant, as if I were already a star. She phoned up somebody and in about three minutes Woody Woodward came out. He put his arm around my shoulder and kind of walked me over to the side of the reception lounge. "Listen, baby, this guy we're seeing is the Camelot A. and R. man. Everybody calls him Superman because he's put together so many hits. He's got a real commercial feel. He can smell a winner a mile away.

He's got about twenty kids lined up waiting to try out for this deal but I persuaded him to see you first. One thing, he had polio when he was a kid. He walks around on crutches, and he's very sensitive about his legs. Don't stare or anything. Okay? Groovy, baby. Let's go."

We walked down a maze of corridors to Superman's office. It was a really terrific place with a huge desk and enormous windows that you could see out of for miles. You could even see LaGuardia Airport, and tiny planes coming in for a landing.

The A. and R. man was sitting behind the huge desk. A. and R. stands for "Artist and Repertory." In a record company, the A. and R. man is the one who really decides which records to make and I guess this one was considered terrific about knowing which records would sell. He was completely bald, as if he had shaved his head. He had hardly any eyebrows, either, and his eyes seemed to stand out like blue eggs. His shoulders and arms were big, the way they usually are with people who walk on crutches. He was wearing a T-shirt that said I LOVE CAMELOT on it. He didn't get up when we came in. I guess it was too much trouble for him. He just stared at me, and after a while he said, "Hmm."

"I told you he was a good-looking kid," Woody said.

Superman stared at me through his big egg-eyes. Then he opened his desk drawer, took out a huge cigar, smelled it, bit off the end, and lit it. "Havana," he said. "Illegal here. No *way* a customs inspector can tell Havana if you take the labels off." He rolled it in his fingers, then he lit it and blew out a huge puff of smoke all over me and Woody. "Have the kid turn sideways, Woody, so I can get a look at his profile."

The way he said it made it sound as if I were a poodle in a dog show. I didn't say anything, but just turned sideways. "Hmm," he said again. "How old is he, Woody?"

"Thirteen," Woody said.

"Hmm," Superman said. "Born the year I went to jail." That was a pretty interesting remark, and I quickly tried to figure out some polite way of asking him more about it, but I couldn't come up with anything in time.

"But he's got the kind of face that could pass for anything from eleven to sixteen," Woody said.

Superman blew smoke all over us. "Maybe twelve. Eleven I doubt. Does he have to shave yet?"

"No," Woody said. "He won't start shaving for years. They mature late in his family." That was a complete lie. I'd already shaved twice.

"I don't know," Superman said.

He stared his egg-eyes at me some more. "He isn't flipping me out with his personality. Have him bop a little, Woody."

"Bop a little, George," Woody said.

"What?" I said. I was getting pretty tired of being in a dog show, and besides, I didn't know what he meant by bopping.

"Give us a little personality."

"Oh," I said. What they wanted me to do was to start talking about something with a lot of gestures and some big phony smiles. You know, say something like, "Well, Mr. Superman, I certainly appreciate this opportunity, wait till I tell the rest of the kids that I actually met you," and stuff like that. Some kids can do that, just walk up to a grown-up and talk to him and tell stories. I can't. They were staring at me, so rapidly I tried to think of something interesting to say. But my mind was blank, and finally I blurted out, "I guess I don't have much personality. I'm just an ordinary kid."

"Hmm," Superman said.

"See, that's his schtick," Woody said. "Just your plain ordinary kid who happens to have all this talent falling out of his ears. The boy next door. Modest. Bashful."

"Hmm," Superman said.

"The kind of kid who's happiest walking down a country road, munching on an apple, or fishing in a creek with a bamboo pole and a bent pin."

"Hmm," Superman said. "Hmm."

"Milking the cows and pitching the hay," Woody said. "Camelot Records' hot new star, George Stable, The Boy Next Door."

"Hmm," Superman said. "Maybe."

"Swinging on a grapevine."

"That's too much Tarzan-time," Superman said. "What we want is Vermont-time."

"You took the words right out of my mouth," Woody said. "Sledding down this old country road with scarf and earmuffs flying."

They went on this way for a while, still pretending that I was a poodle at a dog show and couldn't understand anything they were saying. I just stood there listening and wondering what Superman went to jail for, and if Woody would buy me a Coke the way he sometimes did. Finally, Superman told Woody to get some test pictures made and we went out of the office and down the elevator. All the way down Woody kept saying, "We're home, baby. I've never seen Superman so excited."

"He didn't seem too excited to me, Woody. All he said was 'Hmm.'"

"You don't know Superman, baby. All he usually ever says is 'Hmm.' But today he was really talking—I mean, using actual words."

"Something might come out of it this time, you mean?"

"Well, look, Georgie, I don't want to make any promises. Everything in this business is a spin of the dice, but I could tell that he loved the concept—George Stable, The Boy Next Door."

"Did you just think that up on the spur of the moment?"

"I had to do something, Georgie, the way you were coming on like a block of wood."

I blushed. "What kind of act would it be?"

"Oh, I'll figure something out." We had got down to the street and were standing there. I was wondering if he would buy me a Coke. Woody took out a cigarette and flicked his lighter at it. Woody is the greatest man in New York at cigarette lighters. He just sort of flicks his wrist and there's the lighter in his hand as if he had dealt it out of his shirtsleeve.

"Listen, Woody," I said. "What did Superman go to jail for?"

"God, Georgie, don't ever bring that up with him."

"No, but I mean, what was he in for?"

"Drugs. He was some kind of big dealer. At least that's the story. He did about three years. But for God's sake, don't bring it up."

"I won't," I said.

"You just worry about the singing, I'll worry about Superman."

"Maybe I won't be good enough," I said.

"Confidence, baby, con-fee-*dence*. We'll get you some shy-type, down-home songs to do. All you'll have to do is stand around and look bashful and stutter."

"That doesn't sound very interesting to me," I said.

He slapped me on the shoulder. "Stay loose, baby. Let me do the worrying. Now go on home. I'll call you when we get the photographer set up."

I was disappointed that he didn't buy me a Coke. I walked over to Sixth Avenue and took the IND subway home. I didn't know what to believe. On one hand, I'd heard all that stuff before—about con-fee-*dence* and somebody liking the concept and so forth. It had never worked out before, so why should it work out now? On the other hand, it seemed to me that if you tried often enough, sooner or later something was bound to work out. The one thing I'd learned about show business was that the dumber the plan sounded, the better a chance it had that somebody would do it. If you went to some record company and said, "Hey, I've got an idea, let's get a really good group together and record a lot of really great songs," everybody would look at you as if you were an idiot and ought to be ashamed of yourself. But if you came up with something really nuts, like recording some group on a hayride in an airplane or something, why everybody would say it was terrific. It was a million-dollar idea which would make show business history.

Well, the idea of George Stable, The Boy Next Door, fit right in with that for dumbness. I mean, I'd spent the whole of my life in the least country place in America: Greenwich Village, the nut center of New York City. I never saw a hen until one time I visited Sinclair when I was eight. It surprised me how big they were—I thought they were more the size of pigeons, which was the only kind of bird I'd ever paid any attention to. In fact, I probably knew less about the country than practically anybody in America because we hardly ever went to the country, even for vacations—Pop was always too broke. Frankly, I didn't mind. I never thought the country was so groovy, there was never anything to do except get beaten at chess by Cousin Sinclair. I guess I'm not the kind of person who gets turned on by trees.

Anyway, because I was exactly the wrong type of person to be George Stable, The Boy Next Door, I figured there was a good chance it would happen. And that meant one thing for sure: I couldn't afford to spend the summer upstate watching Cousin Sinclair be perfect.

CHAPTER TWO

OU MIGHT HAVE read about me in a book called *The Teddy Bear Habit*, which I wrote when I was twelve. You probably think it's pretty nutty for a twelve-year-old kid to write a book, and I guess it is. What happened was, because of my own dumbness, I got into a terrible mess with some criminals and almost got killed. I mean, really, I almost got killed, but fortunately I got saved at the last minute. A lot of it had to do with this teddy bear I had. I was sort of hung up on it. I mean, I would carry it around with me, especially when I had to do something that made me nervous. In the end the teddy bear got burned up by one of the criminals. To be perfectly honest,

I'm sort of ashamed of that book, *The Teddy Bear Habit*. Not ashamed of the book so much, but of exposing to everybody that I carried a teddy bear around with me when I was twelve. Of course, I got over that when my teddy bear was burned up. Although, to tell the truth, I still have a teddy bear key chain that my Pop gave to me, just a little fuzzy bear on a chain. He felt sorry about my teddy bear being burned up, and he gave me the key chain. I kind of like having it. Of course, since I got over my teddy bear habit I don't carry the key chain around with me all the time. Carrying around a thing that big in your pocket is a pain. I keep it on my bureau; I just like to look at it sometimes.

Anyway, you probably haven't read that book, so I'd better tell you something about me. The first thing is that I live in Greenwich Village, the Bohemian part of New York, which is just a fancy way of saying that it's full of nuts and whackos. There are lots of painters and writers and actors and so forth who don't have to be nuts, but usually are. Then there are the leftover hippies, who live in these little stores and spend most of their time out on the sidewalk. Honest, they sleep out there and eat their meals out there and play chess there—little kids and mothers and fathers and everybody. Sometimes I go over and talk to them. They're pretty interesting, but to be frank about it, it doesn't appeal to me too much to see them eating out there on the sidewalk with the flies all around and these dirty dogs and cats they have hanging around.

Then we have around the Village people who are *totally* out to lunch. I mean, guys wearing witches' hats and carrying shepherds' poles, people who walk backward, and ones who give long speeches in the park to midair. And the drug addicts. And then of course all the normal people.

I count Pop and me as normal people, but maybe I shouldn't be so sure about Pop. We live on West Fourth Street near where it meets with Cornelia Street and Sixth Avenue. We've lived there all my life. My mother died when I was a baby, just practically born, and my father's had to raise me by himself. I hear a lot about that. He says, "I'm trying to be a father and a mother to you, George, and it isn't easy." To be honest, for him it seems to be impossible. Sometimes he's a good mother and gets up and makes me scrambled eggs or pancakes or something for breakfast, but a lot of the time he just lies there in bed—he sleeps on a daybed in the living room—and shouts out that it's almost eight o'clock and if I don't get up immediately I'll be late for school, which never struck me as a big enough disaster to go shouting around about. And sometimes he gets over to the Laundromat on Monday the way he says he's going to, but about half the time he doesn't, so by Wednesday morning I don't have any clean underwear or socks and my jeans are beginning to look pretty bad, although I admit it would help if I didn't wipe my hands on them so often.

So I say, "Pop, I haven't got any clean underpants," and he says, "Oh hell," which isn't a very good explanation, and I say, "What'll I wear?" and he says, "You have to remind me of these things, George. I can't keep a lot of petty details in my head when I'm trying to make a living, and besides it seems to me that you're old enough to wash out a few things in the sink for yourself." And I say, "Well, I would have, except that you said you were going to the Laundromat on Monday," and he says, "Next time when you take a bath throw a few things into the tub with you and let them soak," and I say, "I never take baths, I take showers, do you want me to go into the shower with my underwear and socks on?" And he says, "I don't want to get into a big wrangle about this, I have a lot of things on my mind this morning," so I go to school with used socks on. I tell you, it isn't much fun having a father for a mother. Who wants to have his father take him up to Gimbels to buy pajamas?

The thing Pop does for a living that keeps his head from being filled up with petty details is draw comic books. His most important cartoon used to be a super hero called Garbage Man, where this mild-mannered advertising executive turned himself into Garbage Man when trouble impended and burned holes in the bad guys with his super smell. Pop still does *Garbage Man,* but now he's more interested in a new one, called *Frankens-Teen*. It's all about a teenager who can turn into a Frankenstein monster whenever he drinks this potent astral fluid which he carries around with him. The minute he drinks it he goes all shuddery and turns into an indestructible monster with stitches all over his face, determined to wreak vengeance on some bad guys. Pop says that sooner or later somebody is bound to buy *Frankens-Teen* for the movies and pay him a million dollars or something, but frankly, I'm not counting on it.

Actually, Pop doesn't want to be a comic strip artist. What he really wants to be is a famous painter like Jackson Pollock or Andy Warhol. Jackson Pollock is dead. He made his pictures by dripping whole cans of paint over huge canvases. They didn't look like anything real, but they weren't supposed to—they were supposed to look like the inside of his mind. Frankly, if my mind were that disorganized I wouldn't let anybody know about it. The pictures Andy Warhol makes look like ordinary things—tomato soup cans and Brillo boxes. Pop used to paint like Jackson Pollock. He used to snap paint on his pictures with a spoon, the way kids snap peas at each other. Now he's changed more over to the Warhol style. For example, he'll paint a picture of a picture. Once he painted this picture of the cover of his own *Frankens-Teen* comic books. It was exactly identical—the same size and color, with the titles and the name of the publisher, just the way they were on the printed one. You could hardly tell them apart. I said, "You mean you painted a picture of a picture you'd already painted?"

"Why not?" he said. "People paint pictures of trees, don't they? Well, that comic book cover is just as real as a tree. It's part of our lives."

"Why didn't you just paste the comic book cover onto the canvas? You could have saved yourself a lot of trouble."

"Aha," he said. "That's the whole point. It's a scathing indictment of contemporary morality. Social commentary in the form of a joke."

"What's so funny about it?" I said. "I think *Frankens-Teen* is funnier."

"That's because you have a juvenile mentality. *Frankens-Teen* is meant to appeal to the twelve-year-old mind."

"I'm thirteen."

"As far as I'm concerned, you're a juvenile," he said. "Wait until this picture makes me rich and famous. I won't give you any of the money."

I thought about saying that he didn't give me any money anyway, but that would just give him an excuse to tell me how lucky I was, New York was full of kids who barely got enough to eat, much less any allowance. I didn't think I could stand that, so I kept my mouth shut.

I don't mean to say that Pop is a bad guy. Sometimes he's pretty nice. I mean, one day he'll remind me of all the poor people there are in New York and threaten to cut off my allowance. The next day I'll ask him for some money for the movies and he'll give me five dollars and tell me to keep the change. But the big problem is this whole thing about how I'm a juvenile and only thirteen and can't be trusted to run my own life and all of that. What difference does it make to him if I get to school late or get bad grades or even flunk out? It's my life, isn't it? Why shouldn't I be allowed to make a mess out of it if I want?

Stanky agreed with me that Pop was too bossy.

"Your parents aren't so bossy," I said. We were lying around his room messing the place up with grape-jelly slushes we made in his blender.

"They don't pay much attention to what I do," he said.

"They aren't always bugging you about something," I said.

"They leave it up to Eloise to bug me." Eloise is their maid.

"Yes, but they let you stay up late if you want to or skip school sometimes."

"That's because I get straight As."

"It wouldn't matter to Pop if I got straight As, he'd still order me to get up and go to school on time," I said.

He took a suck on his grape-jelly slush. "Boy, are these grape-jelly slushes terrible," he said.

"I think we put in too much vanilla," I said.

"You have to put lots of vanilla in slushes," he said. "Otherwise they don't taste like slushes."

"Well, anyway," I said.

"The thing is, George, my parents and your father are different. My parents just don't worry about me very much, they figure I'm okay and they do their own thing. But your father worries about you all the time because you haven't got any mother."

"I might get a mother," I said, "and I don't think it's going to make any difference."

"It probably will. At least maybe she'll take your clothes to the Laundromat."

"She has to work," I said. "More likely it'll end up I'll have to take *her* clothes to the Laundromat."

"When are they getting married?" Stanky said.

"I don't know," I said. "They keep arguing about it. Pop says, 'What the hell's the big rush about getting married, it might spoil everything,' and she says, 'We've been going around together for three years and I'm not getting any younger.' I think it'll be pretty soon, though. Pop's getting tense."

Pop's girlfriend was named Denise Rothwell. She was an editor at Smash Comics, which is where Pop met her. Smash Comics is the company Pop works for. I don't mean he goes there every day. He's a freelancer and mainly works at home, although sometimes he has to go up there and fix up something on one of his comic strips that he supposedly did wrong. It makes him furious when his own girlfriend calls up and tells him something is wrong with his comic strip. He shouts over the phone, "You're just being picky, Denise; cut it out, will you," but he has to go up there and fix it or he won't get paid. Pop is broke a lot and always needs to get paid.

Denise Rothwell believes in Women's Lib. So do I. Pop says he believes in it, too, but he doesn't really. I mean, he believes in it when it comes time for Denise to pay for her own movie ticket or her share of dinner when we go to a restaurant, which isn't too often, but when it actually comes down to the question of who's boss, they usually end up having a fight. Pop says, "You're just trying to make an issue of it," and Denise says, "No I'm not, you're being bossy," and they end up not speaking to each other for a day until they calm down and go down to Fidelio's for a drink and work out an agreement. I'm usually in favor of Denise. Anybody who's trying to get liberated from Pop, that's the side I'm on.

It may seem like I'm getting off the track, but you have to know about Pop and Denise to understand what happened. Around last March or something they had their usual fight about getting married. To calm Denise down Pop said they ought to go to Paris. Of course I wasn't supposed to be hearing it, I was supposed to be asleep. But we have a kind of small apartment—just a big living room with a skylight where Pop works and has his daybed, and a tiny kitchen and a bathroom and my room, which isn't so big, either. If anybody out in the living room is talking in loud tones it keeps me awake. At least if it's interesting it keeps me awake. If they're talking about politics or some philosophical question I can usually fall asleep without much trouble. But this was interesting and it kept me awake.

Pop said, "We'll go to Paris and have the honeymoon first and then get married later—sometime in the fall when the weather is cooler."

"What does cool weather have to do with getting married?" Denise said, which I thought was a pretty good question.

"Oh," Pop said, "you don't want to get married in the heat of the summer."

"May I point out that it was twenty-six degrees this morning. Is that cool enough for marriage?"

"Stop changing the subject," Pop said. "The question is, what about going to Paris?"

I could tell that Denise wanted to go to Europe all right. She hadn't been there since her junior year in college, she said. Pop had lived in Paris for a year once, before he married my mother, but he hadn't been back since. So Denise shut up about getting married and they talked about it some more and after a few days they came up with a plan which they didn't want to tell me about right away, as I might be upset.

The plan was that they'd go right after school ended. They wanted to go for four weeks. Being a freelancer, Pop could take a vacation whenever he saved up some money, which he usually didn't. Denise would take a leave of absence. As for me, they were going to stuff me off upstate at my uncle Ned's house with my cousin Sinclair. Man, did I hate Cousin Sinclair. Cousin Sinclair thought he was perfect, which maybe I could have stood except that his parents agreed with him. They were always saying, "See the marvelous story Sinclair wrote," or "The music teacher says that Sinclair's the most brilliant flute student he's ever had," or, "Have you seen Sinclair's painting that won the school prize?" Well, the story would be some crap about a little lost child that got raised in the woods by elves, and the picture would be seagulls swooping over the waves and as far as the flute was concerned

Cousin Sinclair was pretty good at lilting airs out of his Little Masterpieces book, but he wasn't going to get very many plays on the A.M. stations. I hate to brag, but the truth is that I'm a better musician than Sinclair, although naturally nobody in his family was going to believe that. Anyway, you can imagine I wasn't very thrilled with the idea of spending half the summer stuffed off upstate. I'd never spent four consecutive weeks with Cousin Sinclair and I was afraid I might murder him before the first week was over.

But what could I do about it? I spent a lot of time thinking about it. It really bothered me. It wasn't fair. Why should I have to suffer just so they could go to Paris? I mean, I had nothing against them going to Paris, they were allowed to do that if they wanted. But why did I have to get stuffed off in upstate New York with Cousin Sinclair?

But I couldn't argue about it until they told me about it. I mean, I wasn't supposed to know yet, so there wasn't anything I could do about it yet. It was hard not to talk about it. A couple of times I almost blurted out something about it. Once they were talking about who was King of England during the war and I almost asked them if they were going to visit London when they were in Europe. Another time, when Pop gave me my measly dollar-fifty allowance, I started to ask him if Uncle Ned was going to pay me my allowance when he was gone. But both times I managed to stop in time; and finally one day Pop said, "Put on a clean shirt, we're going out to dinner with Denise," and I knew they were going to tell me about it. It was about time; it was hard keeping their secret from them.

We went to the Open Hart, which is their usual restaurant. It's just a place with booths and red-checked tablecloths and candles stuck in Chianti bottles. The air conditioner hardly ever works and there's usually a big cloud of grease pouring out of the kitchen and it hasn't got any class at all, but they like it because it's cheap. I don't care. All I ever eat is a big plate of spaghetti and meatballs with a side order of garlic bread and two big Cokes, which Pop says rots your teeth.

So we went there and as soon as Pop ordered a bottle of wine and took a big gulp he told me that he and Denise were going to Paris. I said, "Gee, I never would have thought you'd do something like that."

"I hope it doesn't come as too much of a shock," Pop said.

I ignored that. "Well look, can Stanky come and stay with me in the apartment while you're gone?"

He and Denise looked at each other. "Well, what I thought was that—"

"I mean, since you're paying for the apartment anyway, we might as well use it. If you sent me upstate or somewhere it would cost all that train fare, and then you'd have to give the people money for my food and some extra in case of emergency."

"What made you think of upstate?" he asked.

"Oh, I don't know," I said. "It was just a place that happened to come to my mind."

"Well, actually, I was thinking you might enjoy being with Sinclair for the summer. There's the lake right there and Uncle Ned will take you waterskiing."

"I flatly refuse," I said. "I will not spend the summer with that turkey Sinclair."

"Oh, don't be unreasonable, George. Sinclair is a perfectly nice kid."

"Cousin Sinclair is a schmuck."

"Don't use that word about your own cousin," he said.

"If he's my cousin why can't I call him what I want?"

"I think we ought to change the subject," Denise said. "Let's talk about it another time."

"Why, Denise?" I said. "If I'm going to have a fight with Pop we might as well get it over now."

"Because it's spoiling my dinner, which I

happen to be paying for. Now if you or your father want to pay for my dinner, I'll consider letting you spoil it."

"Very witty, Denise," Pop said.

"I suppose you're going to gang up on me, now," she said.

"Do I have to listen to you two fight all the time?" I said. I meant it as a joke, but instead it was a mistake.

They both stared at me. Finally Pop said, "Now, look, George."

I picked up the menu and pretended to read it. "I guess I'll have my usual spaghetti and meatballs," I said.

They stared at me some more and I tried to hide down behind the menu. I could feel their eyes charging through the air at me. Finally Pop said, "All right. Let's be cheerful and have a pleasant dinner. We'll talk about it later."

So we talked about it a couple of days later when Pop and I were having dinner at home. This time I had my arguments all worked out.

"Here's the thing," I said. "I promise to keep the apartment clean and I promise I'll eat vegetables and stuff and not live on peanut butter and jelly sandwiches and do the laundry and all that. And if there's an emergency or anything, I can go over to Stanky's. I mean, if I got sick or something like that. So there isn't anything for you to worry about. That way when you get back the place will be clean and all ready for you."

"There's more to it, George. For one thing, I expect to sublet the place. I can probably get three hundred dollars for the four weeks. There are always visiting professors at New York University who are looking for places to rent while they're in New York. I can't afford to pass up the money."

"Oh," I said. "Well, how much will it cost for my train fare up to Sinclair's?"

"About four dollars each way."

"Oh," I said. I thought about it. "Well, what about my food?"

"I'd have to feed you anyway, George."

"Well, suppose I promised to live on peanut butter sandwiches, that would save you a lot."

"You just promised *not* to live on peanut butter sandwiches."

"Well, listen, Pop, what if the record deal with Woody goes through? I mean, if that happened I couldn't be upstate with Sinclair, I'd have to be in New York."

"George, don't get your hopes up over that. It isn't going to happen."

"Woody said it was hot," I said.

"Woody always says everything is hot."

"But suppose."

"We'll cross that bridge when we come to it."

"How can we cross that bridge if we come to it when you're in Paris?"

"A couple of weeks isn't going to matter, George."

"But what if it did? I mean, what if I had to make some tests or something right away. Could I—"

"George, I'm tired of arguing about this. Sinclair isn't all that bad. I remember one summer a few years ago when you had a good time with him."

"That was five years ago," I said. "Besides, who wants to spend four weeks getting beaten at chess by somebody who thinks he's perfect?"

"Oh, come on, George. All that fresh country air and swimming and waterskiing. You'll find lots to do."

"What's hot about fresh air?" I said. But it wasn't any use and I knew it. Pop had made up his mind and that was that. It made me mad as hell. It just wasn't fair, getting shoved off with Cousin Sinclair just so Pop could have a good time. I wasn't asking him to do me any favors, I was willing to take care of myself and even pay for my own food and all that. But the real truth was, it didn't have anything to do with subletting the apartment or Sinclair being a big load of fun. The whole idea was that Pop didn't think I was old enough to take care of myself.

That was what it was all about, and it made me sore as hell. What right had he to tell me what to do? Why should I have to obey his every whim like some slave?

CHAPTER THREE

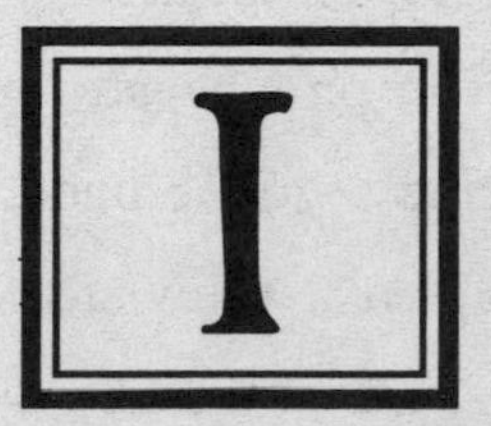

I DON'T KNOW WHY it is, but nothing ever happens one at a time. You go along for weeks being bored and wishing something would happen. Finally, you get up a plan to bike out to Fire Island with somebody and that turns out to be the Saturday that Mr. Stanky wants to take you out on his friend's power cruiser; and just when you're trying to make up your mind about that, somebody gives your father tickets to the ball game.

That's what was happening to me. First it was Pop and Denise going to Paris, and then me going to Cousin Sinclair's. Then it was Woody Woodward's new means for being rich and famous.

I guess I ought to explain how I got into the music business, or anyway, how I was always about to be getting into the music business.

When I was around eight Pop made me take singing lessons—not folk singing or anything, but arias and stuff like that. Later on I began to take guitar lessons from a crazy guy named Wiggsy and I ended up being on a television program for about six seconds and got to be a hero around my school for ten days.

Well, then it got to be a big question of was I talented and should I go on to make music my career. I kept having these long discussions with Pop about it. It seemed to me that I was pretty young to decide something like that, but Mr. Smythe-Jones, my aria teacher, told Pop that you have to begin early to produce a trained voice. I didn't know what to do; but finally this guy named Woody Woodward got into it. Woody Woodward is part of a company called Woodward and Hayes, which is in the business of organizing groups for television and radio and records and all that. It isn't just rock groups. Say, for example, you have this television program and want some background music for the murder, why they'll put together a group and tape up some murder music for you. Or suppose you want to put out a commercial where some phony folk singer comes on and sings about how marvelous your chewing gum is, Woodward and Hayes will arrange for that. And of course they do a lot of regular records, too—you know, they'll get together a group to put out Golden Oldies from last year, or theme music from monster movies or stuff like that.

Well, what happened was that after I was on that television program for those six seconds, Woody Woodward decided to sign me to a contract. It sounds like a big deal, but it wasn't. All it meant was that he'd give me some advice and if I got rich and famous he'd take half the money. Of course Pop got all into a thing about it. He hates popular music. The only kind of music he likes is classical—Bach and Vivaldi and that stuff. He keeps it going on the radio all day long when he's drawing *Garbage Man* or *Frankens-Teen.* He keeps trying to get me to like it, too. That would be all right with me. I'm perfectly willing to like Bach, but I just can't seem to do it. How can you like something if you don't like it? For example, I can't stand clams, but one day at a restaurant everybody told me I didn't know what I was missing, so I tried one, and I almost threw up. I would *like* to like clams, but I don't; it's the same with Bach, and what can I do about it?

Anyway, when Woody Woodward wanted to sign me up he went down to talk to Pop about it. Pop puffed around and said that the music business was a jungle; he wanted me exposed to finer music instead of that awful uproar. Finally Woody took Pop out to Fidelio's for a drink, and talked about how much money I could make, and in the end Pop agreed, provided I would go on with Mr. Smythe-Jones, my aria teacher. Woody got me a good guitar teacher and I began to study some music theory and after a while, between all these lessons, I got to where I wasn't too bad.

But to be honest, after two years it was getting to be a big pain in the butt. First there was my singing lesson with Mr. Smythe-Jones, where I had to honk away at "The Donkey Serenade" for an hour, with Smythe-Jones saying, "Into*na*tion, George, intonation, *please*" every time I went flat, which was pretty often. Then there was a half hour a week on the guitar lesson, which wasn't so bad, except that he really loaded me down on the practicing. On top of it, there was my theory lesson, an hour every two weeks, where I was supposed to bring in a sixteen-bar waltz or something I'd written so we could go over it. I was terrible at that, worse than at singing in tune. The only part of the whole thing I liked at all was the guitar, because usually we'd be working on some real song. But I was supposed to practice scales and chords a half hour a day, too. At first it was kind of interesting studying all that music, but by this time I was sick of having to go to my lessons all the time, and bored with practicing and fed up with getting shouted at for not practicing, which was what usually happened. And I would have quit the whole thing, except that every time I was about to get up my nerve to tell Woody Woodward that I didn't want to be a musician, I just wanted to be an ordinary kid, he would come up with a big deal that was going to make me rich and famous. First there was some guy who was going to put together a kids' group for some television show; but that was the year that cowboy shows were big on television and nobody wanted a kids' group. Then there was the idea for a group imitating the Cowsills, where I was going to be part of a phony family named the Sheepmeadows, but just as that was getting started the big leader of it got busted for dope and that ended that. Then I was going to be in that murder movie for about a minute, and I practiced for six weeks on a minute's worth of music, which believe me was pretty boring; but they never made the movie.

Each time Woody came up with something like this I would get interested in music again, and then it would peter out and I would think about quitting again until Woody came up with the next means of getting rich and famous.

I was over at Stanky's, messing up his room with some peanut butter slushes we made in his blender.

"George, what'll you do if Woody wants you to come to New York for something?"

"I don't know," I said.

"How far is it?"

"Oh, it isn't too far. I guess you can get there in a couple of hours on the train. But that isn't the problem, the problem is that if I have to come back to New York for something, Uncle Ned probably won't let me. I mean, he'll say it doesn't sound sensible. That's my Uncle Ned's thing, saying that things don't sound sensible. It gives him a big charge to tell people things they want to do aren't sensible. Then he'll write to Pop about it, and Pop will say wait until he gets back, four weeks isn't going to hurt anybody."

"What'll Woody say?"

"He'll be furious. He'll go find somebody else to be The Boy Next Door."

"Maybe you'll have to run away."

"Maybe I will," I said. I didn't want to make it too definite, so in case I chickened out I wouldn't have to admit it, but could say I changed my mind for some reason I'd make up. "I mean, if I don't get to be George Stable, The Boy Next Door, I might as well stay up at Cousin Sinclair's and suffer."

"Probably," he said. "Boy, are these peanut butter slushes terrible. I think we ought to go back to banana ones."

"Why did you have to pick this year to go to music camp?"

"Because my parents are going to Los Angeles, that's why."

"How come you don't have any Cousin Sinclair to get shoved off with?"

"I do. There's my cousin Philip. He's almost as perfect as your cousin Sinclair."

"Nobody's as perfect as Cousin Sinclair. I'll go nuts spending four weeks with him. It isn't fair. Pop doesn't spend four weeks with Uncle Ned.

"Why should he? Your uncle Ned is your mother's brother, not his."

"If I can't have a mother, why do I have to be stuck with having a cousin?" I said.

"Some cousins are okay."

"Let's stop talking about cousins," I said. "I can't stand the subject anymore. The main thing is, how am I going to get out of it?"

"You better resign yourself, George."

"What about George Stable, The Boy Next Door?" I said.

"You said these things never work out."

"But this one might. I have a feeling it might."

"You've had that feeling every time," Stanky said.

I hit him on the arm. "Sorry about that," I said.

But I couldn't think of anything and Stanky couldn't think of anything either, so I just went on home trying to figure out why it was always me who got cheated instead of somebody else.

Pop was cooking supper. For somebody who had been cooking for thirteen years he wasn't very good, but I didn't mind. He made stew okay and macaroni and cheese and these weird casseroles where he'd heave everything in the icebox into a dish and mix it up with rice and tomato sauce—those casseroles were pretty interesting because you never knew what you were going to stumble on under the tomato sauce. Most of Pop's food didn't have the same interest: spaghetti and then burned hamburgers and then limp hot dogs and spaghetti again. There was one advantage to it, though. Pop didn't worry much about balanced diets so I never had to force down a lot of liver or codfish or lovely green salads the way Stanky did.

Tonight he was cooking one of his weird casseroles. "Where have you been?"

"Shooting baskets," I said. There wasn't any reason to lie about being at Stanky's, I just wanted to from being mad.

"Good," he said. "It'll give you an appetite. I'm making a superb supper, a truly gourmet confection." He was pretty cheerful because he was going to Europe in a few days.

"Will I be able to eat it?" I said.

"It'll tickle your tonsils." There were some noodles cooking on the stove. He took them over to the sink and poured off the water. About half the noodles fell into the sink, but he just picked them up with his fingers and heaved them back into the pan. Then he took the pan over to the icebox and stood there with the door open, peering around. "Aha," he said. "Meatballs."

There were three old meatballs sitting on a saucer. He dumped them into the noodles. Then he found a dish of leftover lima beans, which he dumped in, too, and some anchovies he had left over from the week before when he and Denise had had some other comic strip artists over for cocktails. Next he found a piece of Parmesan cheese and two wrinkled hot dogs and half a bologna sandwich.

"There's some strawberry ice cream in the freezer," I said.

"No, no, mustn't overdo it," he said.

"What about that pot holder by the sink?"

"George, in cooking it's important to distinguish between the food and the utensils."

"I'm glad you told me that," I said. "Otherwise I wouldn't have known."

"It's a rule I always follow," he said.

"What about the time we found the spoon in the marble cake?"

"Somebody must have dropped it in when I wasn't looking."

"Yes, indeedy," I said. "Probably the dog."

"Exactly. The dog."

"We don't have a dog."

"I knew that all along," he said.

I was getting tired of this. "When will it be ready?"

"Ten minutes. It just has to heat up." He got a big spoon and stirred everything around in the noodles—the hot dog, the lima beans, the anchovies and all—and shoved the dish in the oven.

"I'm going in my room to read," I said.

"Wait a minute, George," he said. "I want to talk to you."

Here it came. "Why do I have to—"

"Now, George. Please don't start arguing. There isn't any other way. I got a letter from your uncle Ned this morning and it's all set. School's out next Wednesday, Denise and I are leaving on Friday, so you have to go up to Sinclair's on Thursday morning."

"Darn it, it's not fair."

"A lot of things in life aren't fair," he said.

"Big deal."

"Watch your tongue," he said. "There's a nine o'clock train leaving from Grand Central. I'll take you up and put you on it. It gets up there at eleven. Uncle Ned and Sinclair will meet you."

There wasn't any point in arguing and I knew it. I didn't want to hear any more about it. "I'll be in my room reading," I said.

So that was that. There wasn't any way out of it. He would put me on the train and Uncle Ned and Aunt Cynthia would capture me when I got off and keep me in prison for four weeks with Cousin Sinclair as the torturer.

And what about George Stable, The Boy Next Door? If I missed out on making a record and getting rich and famous because of Sinclair, I'd kill somebody—probably myself. I knew that before I went I'd better call up Woody Woodward and find out if the idea was hot, which would mean that it wasn't going to happen, or red hot, which would mean that it might happen sometime around Christmas, or so hot that it was on fire, which would mean that it might happen in a couple of months. So the next afternoon when Pop was up at Smash Comics, having his mistakes pointed out to him by Denise, I called up Woody.

"I was just checking to see if anything was happening," I said.

"It's hotter than hot, baby," he said. "It's fire engine time."

"Great," I said. "That means they might want to get going by fall."

"Fall? Georgie this is moving like a jet of live steam. You aren't going off to camp or something, are you?"

"No," I said. "The only thing is, I might be upstate visiting my cousin for a while."

"For a while? How long is that?"

"Oh, well. About a week I guess."

"A whole week?" he said.

"A weekend, I meant to say."

"Well, okay, but keep in touch. I may need you all of a sudden. When Superman moves, he moves fast."

I hung up and began to pray that Superman didn't decide to move for four weeks.

So the days went by. On Wednesday school got out. I packed an old beat-up suitcase Pop had on the closet shelf with my clothes and that night I went over to say good-bye to Stanky. "You louse," I said. "Going to music camp when I have to be tortured by Sinclair."

"Sorry about that," he said. "Did you call up Woody Woodward?"

"Yeah," I said. "It's hotter than a jet of live steam."

"What does that mean?"

"I don't know," I said. "Probably nothing. You never can find out what anything means in this business."

"What'll you do if they want you to make a record when you're up at Cousin Sinclair's?"

"Kill myself."

"Tell me what you want on your gravestone."

"I have to go," I said, "or Pop will have a hemorrhage. Give me your address. If you're lucky I'll write you a letter with all the news from Sinclair's."

"If I'm lucky I'll get a postcard with your name on it," he said. But he gave me his address on a scrap of paper and I said so long and left. And the next morning Pop took me up to Grand Central to put me on the train. It made my heart sink just to see it sitting there, and for a minute I thought about running—just taking off through the crowd and disappearing someplace before Pop could catch me. But I wouldn't ever do something like that. So Pop bought me a Coke and a bag of potato chips and a Heinlein book, which shows that he felt sorry for me, because he usually says that science fiction is intellectually feckless. The door clanged shut. I waved good-bye and so did he, and the train pulled out, and I was on my way to jail. I felt terrible and suddenly I realized that I'd never been away from Pop for more than a few days at a time, except that two weeks I was at camp when I was eight.

CHAPTER FOUR

FTER A WHILE I cheered up a little. We went up through the Bronx and then out into the country, and I looked out the window at the sights. When I got tired of looking out the window, I drank my Coke and spread potato chips all over my shirt, and read my Heinlein book. We were only a half an hour late getting there. Uncle Ned and Sinclair were standing in the waiting room watching me get off the train; and they drove me out to their house, which is in a little town called Pawling. Their house is a kind of old-fashioned, farm-housey kind of place. It was pretty nice if you liked that stuff. Uncle Ned was a math teacher at the high school, which

partly explains why Sinclair was such a schmuck. If your father is a schoolteacher you have to be perfect or it reflects on him. I mean, what a disappointment you'd be if you weren't perfect.

Well, the first day was okay because it was sort of new and that was interesting, but by the second day it was beginning to go downhill. Uncle Ned was sort of fat and bald. He had a habit of sitting behind his newspaper on the front porch and grunting. I mean, every time he came across something in the newspaper that excited him, he'd give this kind of grunty "ummpphh." Sometimes Aunt Cynthia would ask, "What's that, Ned?" and he'd report the big news that they were breaking ground for the new supermarket on Wednesday or that there was a foot of snow on Mount Washington still. But mostly he didn't explain the "ummpphhs." He just pushed them out and let them hang there, and then after a while he'd push out another one, and let that hang there, too.

But Uncle Ned was no problem, he didn't take much interest in me; and Aunt Cynthia was away at various church things and library meetings most of the time when she wasn't cooking, so she wasn't much of a problem, either. The problem was guess who. As I said, the first day wasn't so bad because of things being new. But the next morning, around the time that Denise and Pop were going out to Kennedy Airport to fly to Paris, he began in on me about his perfectness. Actually, it was my own fault. Like a dummy, just to be polite and make conversation over our scrambled eggs, I asked him when he got out of school.

"Last week," he said. "We haven't got our report cards yet but I imagine I'll get straight As. As usual."

"That must be kind of dull," I said. "I mean, where's the suspense if you always know you're going to get As in everything?"

"I can't help it," he said. "I just seem to know the answers to all the questions. Of course, I've cultivated good study habits. The subject I hate most is Latin, so I always do that right after I come home from school to get it out of the way. Then I practice the flute. It refreshes my mind. Then I do my exercises. I sent away for a bodybuilding course. The exercises are tailored to develop each muscle of the body individually. You can get muscle-bound if you're not careful."

"That certainly would be a shame," I said. I felt guilty about being sarcastic, but I couldn't help it any more than Sinclair could help getting As.

He didn't notice, though. "I do push-ups and sit-ups and work out with the dumbbells. You can borrow the book if you want. You're supposed to do the exercises in a certain sequence, though. Otherwise you might get muscle-bound."

"I wouldn't want that," I said. "Please pass the maple syrup."

"Maple syrup? On your eggs?"

"Sure," I said. "Don't you ever put maple syrup on your eggs? It's my usual thing." That was a big fat lie. I'd never put maple syrup on my eggs in my life; I was just trying to get even. So I poured the syrup on, and took a bite. It tasted awful, but I acted like it was delicious. "So what else do you do for fun?"

"Oh, I'm afraid I've been sort of neglecting my homework. I've got into another project. I'm building a computer out in the barn."

"A computer?" I wasn't sure I believed that.

"Sure," he said. "All you have to know is a little calculus. You can see it after breakfast. I'll let you help if you think you can be careful. It's awfully delicate, you know."

"I'll try my best," I said.

It turned out to be true about the computer. They have a barn out back of the house which used to have horses and stuff in it fifty years ago when the place was still a farm or whatever it was, but now they used it for a garage and a place to stash the lawn mower and so forth.

And up in the loft, where the hay used to be, Sinclair had a workbench and soldering irons and tiny screwdrivers and boxes full of radio tubes and transistors and wires and a lot of other stuff I didn't recognize. Beside it, sitting on its own table, was this huge mass of electronic things stuck together. "Does it work, Sinclair?"

"It isn't finished yet," he said, "but it'll do quadratic equations already. Watch." He pushed down some buttons he'd got from an old adding machine and after a while the machine began to click and hum and a piece of paper curled out of a hole in the side. Sinclair looked it over. "Right on the nose," he said.

"How can you be sure, Sinclair?"

"I did the problem in my head first."

"You mean you can do math in your head faster than the computer can?"

"Oh, no," he said. "Just simple things. Here, now if you want to help me, I'll show you what to do."

"Maybe you'd rather shoot baskets," I said.

"Oh, no," he said. "My exercise course says that kind of workout doesn't do you any good—it just builds up the legs at the expense of the rest of your musculature."

I was about to explain that maybe we could do it just for fun and never mind building up our musculature. But I didn't; there didn't seem to be much use in trying to explain about fun to Sinclair.

So that was the way it went. In the mornings we worked on Sinclair's computer. That is, I sat around watching him work on it and maybe about every half an hour I held a wire with a pair of pliers while he soldered it. In the afternoons I watched him do his exercises. In the evenings the fun was listening to Uncle Ned grunt along behind his paper. Oh, I'm exaggerating. Sometimes Uncle Ned took us over to some lake they have there and we would go swimming or waterskiing. I got the hang of waterskiing pretty quickly and in about an hour

I was as good as Sinclair, which made him sore. "Your musculature is probably more advanced than mine at this stage," he explained.

"Get stuffed, Sinclair," I said. "I'm just a better athlete than you are."

"Better is a relative term," he said.

"Yes, indeedy," I said. "And you're my relative." It was a terrible joke, but I didn't care. It was nice being better than Sinclair at something. To be honest about it, I figured I was really smarter than Sinclair, too. But I didn't say so; I didn't have any proof.

Actually, sometimes I felt a little sorry for Sinclair. In one way it would be terrific to go around knowing that you were perfect, but in another way he seemed kind of out of it. He'd got himself computerized into doing everything right, and what was the fun in that? I figured someday I would try to persuade him into doing something bad for a change—eating with his fingers or leaving his clothes on the floor. I figured that if I told him it was mentally healthy for him to be rebellious every once in a while he might accept it. It would be something to relieve the boredom. But it wasn't going to be easy to persuade him to stop being perfect. He'd got into the habit of it, and a habit like that is hard to break.

But I had something more important on my mind than Sinclair's perfectness. I kept worrying about Woody Woodward. It wasn't likely that the thing was really going like a jet of live steam, but there was always the chance. Some way I had to get a phone call in to New York. I didn't want Uncle Ned or Aunt Cynthia listening in on the call. So I had to wait until everybody was out of the house. As far as Aunt Cynthia went, that was easy; she was gone most of the time to one of her meetings. But Uncle Ned was another problem. Because school was out he was around a lot—and of course, Sinclair was around every waking minute.

But I had to do it, and I kept watching for

my chance. Finally, about the fifth day I was there, we were out in the barn working on the computer, when I heard Uncle Ned's VW start up. Aunt Cynthia was already out somewhere.

"Sinclair," I said, "I have to go to the bathroom."

"Hurry up," he said. "I want to get all these wires soldered so we can test some problems in analytic geometry."

I climbed down out of the loft and ran into the house. The phone was in the front hall. I found the phone book and worked out the numbers for dialing New York, and put the call through. There was the usual humming and buzzing and then the receptionist came on and said, "Woodward and Hayes."

"Is Woody around?" I asked. "This is George Stable."

"Oh boy," she said. "Where have you been? He's been going nuts looking for you."

A cold chill went over the back of my head, and in about five seconds Woody was on.

"George, I've been trying to get hold of you for days. Where the hell are you?"

"Up in Pawling."

"Well, get your little tail down here as fast as you can. This thing is hotter than molten lava. I want you in my office this afternoon at two o'clock *punto.*"

"I—"

"Don't start stammering on me now, George. I've put two years into this, baby. Just be here."

CHAPTER FIVE

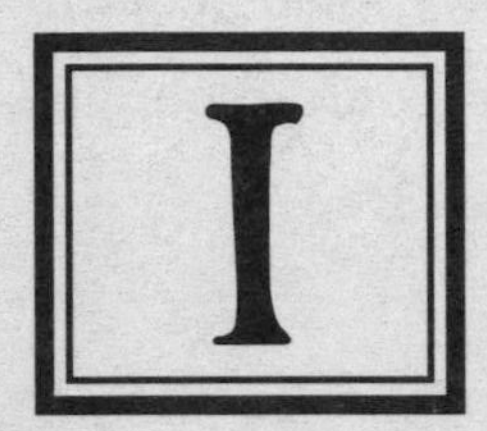

I PUT DOWN THE phone, feeling sort of dizzy and faint. There were a lot of different thoughts swinging around in my mind, but they were coming and going so fast I couldn't catch hold of any of them long enough to know what it was about. I just stood there like that, completely disorganized for I don't know how long. Then I heard Sinclair shout from the barn, "Hey George, hurry up."

I ran upstairs to the back bathroom, which faced out toward the barn, and put my head out the window. "Just a sec," I shouted. "I don't feel too good. I think I got a bug or something."

"Well, hurry," he shouted.

I was still pretty dazed. Of course just because Woody said it was going like molten lava didn't mean anything. In my experience, there were always plenty of firemen around to put out these blazes. It wasn't the first time Woody had screamed at me to be in his office at two o'clock, *punto,* either. Nothing had happened those times, so why would anything happen now?

But, I don't know, it felt different. And what was I going to do? The obvious thing would be to find Uncle Ned, explain to him what it was all about, and get him to put me on the train for New York. But knowing Uncle Ned, the first thing he'd do would be to put out a few surprised grunts, and then he'd say, "George, it doesn't seem sensible to me to send a boy your age off by himself on something like this." Then he'd call Woody, and Woody would find out that I was supposed to be locked up in Sinclair State Pen for the rest of the summer. Or he'd call Pop in Paris, and Pop would hit the ceiling. No, any way you looked at it, being honest with Uncle Ned would only make a mess out of things. It was clear that I was going to have to do a lot of lying over the next little while. Of course, the other thing I could do would be to call up Woody and tell *him* the truth; but that would only bring on a big mess, too. What's the point of telling the truth if all you get out of it are big messes?

The main thing was that I had to get down to New York to find out what was going on. By this afternoon, the chances were that it wouldn't be hotter than molten lava anymore; it'd be just plain old hot, and I could come back to Pawling and forget about it until the next time the volcano overflowed, which would most likely be sometime after next Christmas. That meant thinking up some excuse for going down to New York for the day. I tried to think of one. Maybe I could say that I suddenly remembered that I had a dentist appointment. Or that Pop had just called,

Denise was sick, and they were coming home. Or that Stanky was delirious and kept calling out my name. But as excuses they weren't any good. Anything I could think of, Uncle Ned would call up whoever it was and find out. There was only one thing to do: take off. I could walk to the train station, or better, I could hitchhike into New York. You never could tell. Uncle Ned or somebody might pass by while I was standing at the station.

I flushed the toilet just in case Sinclair had been listening, ran back out to the barn, and climbed up into the loft.

"Listen, Sinclair. I just remembered I have to register for my tutoring school today. In New York."

"Tutoring school? I didn't know you had to go to tutoring school?"

"Sure," I said. "I flunked practically everything last year.

"You have to go down to New York? How could you forget an important thing like that?"

"I forget a lot of important stuff," I said. "I wouldn't have remembered it even now, but this friend of mine just called up to remind me."

"I didn't hear the phone ring," he said.

"You probably missed it. I happened to go by the phone just as it started to ring. It hardly rang at all."

"I still think I would have heard it."

"Not all the way out here you wouldn't. Anyway, this kid said that they changed the date for registering and I have to do it tomorrow."

"How did they get our phone number up here?" He was pretty suspicious.

"Oh, naturally I gave it to this other friend of mine, Everett Stanky. So I figure what I'd better do is take off right away, so I won't foul it up or anything."

He stared at me. "You mean you're going to New York right now?"

"Sure, why not? I'll just hitch down."

"I'll call my father."

"Oh, I don't want to bother him. I'll just go and you tell him I'll be back tonight."

"I think I should call my father."

"Don't bother, Sinclair. Just tell him what happened."

But I didn't trust him. I climbed down out of the loft, raced into the house, and began changing my clothes.

Then I heard Sinclair open the back door. I knew he was coming in to call up his father. So I charged downstairs, out of the house, and onto their road. I didn't know much about Pawling except that there was a big main road to New York just outside of the town. So I trotted out there and began hitchhiking, and about ten minutes later somebody picked me up.

"Where you going?" he said.

"New York," I said.

He gave me a look. I guess he thought it was pretty funny for a kid my age to be hitching to New York. "My father sure is going to be sore.

He gave me four dollars for my train ticket, but I lost it."

"Where you coming from?"

"I've been staying here with my cousin."

"Your cousin?"

"Their name is Stanky. Everett Stanky. Maybe you know them?"

"No, I don't think so," he said. But he seemed satisfied with my story. In telling a lie the basic thing is not to make yourself look too good. I mean, if you want to put it out that you're a big basketball star, don't say that you made the high school team when you were a freshman and averaged thirty points a game the first year. Instead, you should say you didn't get to start regularly until the end of your freshman year. I said, "I'm pretty worried about what Pop's going to say when I tell him I lost the money and had to hitch."

"Why tell him?"

"Oh, I couldn't do that. I never lie to Pop." But that was making me seem too good, so to make it a little more believable I said, "I mean, I don't lie to Pop too much."

So that was all right; and we talked about sports and he drove me into New York. He parked the car in a lot on Forty-second Street and I walked over to Times Square and got a couple of hot dogs smeared up with mustard and ketchup. It was twelve-thirty already. I killed some time walking around, looking at the advertisements for the porno films around Times Square, and then I went up to Woodward and Hayes to find out how on fire everything was.

Woody just shook his head when he saw me. "Baby, you sure are a pain in the butt. I called your home and some chick said you'd gone to Europe. What are they, crazy or something?"

"Pop went to Europe," I said. "He sublet the apartment."

"Where are you staying?"

"With my cousin upstate."

"Upstate? How far?"

"Oh, it isn't far. It only takes about an hour on the train."

He whipped out his pen. "Lemme have the address and phone number so you don't get lost again."

But I didn't want Woody getting into any conversation with Uncle Ned. "I forget the telephone number. I'll get it next time."

"All right, what's the address?"

Or write any letters, either. "I . . . ummm . . ."

"Don't tell me you forgot the address of where you're living?"

"Well, it's just this little town. I know where their house is."

"I don't suppose this little town has a name," he said.

"Pawling."

"Pawling?" He looked suspicious. "That's two or three hours up, isn't it?"

"Oh no, it's only around an hour on the train. I don't remember exactly, though."

"How did you get into town?"

"I hitched."

"Hitched?"

"Yes. My Uncle Ned gave me money for the train ticket, but I lost it."

"George, how could you lose the train money between the house and the station?"

I blushed. "Well, actually I didn't lose it. I owed it to some guy and he saw me at the train station and made me give it to him. He was a pretty big guy."

"How come you owed this big guy money?"

I was beginning to get pretty nervous; I had a lot of lies out and I was beginning to lose track of them. "Well, see, he let me ride his motorbike and I tipped over and busted his taillight."

Woody shook his head. "You lead a complicated life, George. All right, now listen, Georgie, this thing is screaming for action like a fire siren. As far as Superman is concerned, all systems are go. He's putting it to the President of Camelot, Mr. Fenderbase. Next fall, Georgie, it could be star-time."

"So I don't have to do anything until September?"

"Are you kidding? We start in right away—new clothes, the haircut, the image, the public relations boys, the whole kit. I'm going to run your tail off from now until Labor Day. I want to know where you are every minute."

"Okay," I said, swallowing.

He leaned back in his chair. "Now, here's the drill. We've got a meeting with Mr. Fenderbase next week. He's the biggy. He wants to get a look at you. Then we're going to cut some experimental demos, just to see what kind of sound we want to aim for. Then after that, we'll try you out in a live situation. Probably we'll fit you in with a short segment in a concert somewhere, just to get audience reaction. And if it's all working in the fall, we'll cut a record, we'll look for some television guest shots, we'll start booking you around the New York area for some exposure. I suppose your old man won't let you drop out of school."

"I don't think he would," I said.

"Well, we'll work that out when the time comes. Maybe you can be tutored. But let's not count our chickens before they hatch. There are a lot of places we can go wrong yet. Meanwhile, be in here Thursday morning at ten. *Punto.*"

So there it was. I left Woodward and Hayes' office, went down on the street, and bought another hot dog smeared up with stuff from a lunch cart just to calm my nerves. Everything about it was scary. I mean, it was scary enough thinking about what I was going to tell Uncle Ned, without having meetings and demo records and concerts to worry about. And I think I'd have just sort of fainted right there, except that I knew there was a pretty good chance that there'd never be any demo records or concerts, or maybe even no meetings with biggies, so there was no point in getting nervous over something that might never happen. So I calmed down a little, walked over to Grand Central, and took a train up to Pawling, trying to work out my excuses. Thursday was two days away. I had time, but I knew I'd better not lay it on Uncle Ned at the last minute.

I got back to Pawling at five-thirty, and walked over to Sinclair's house, feeling pretty scared. I had a story figured out, but I didn't know if it would work. Sinclair was out front mowing the lawn, and he stopped the minute he saw me come up the street.

"Boy, are you in trouble," he said. "I knew you would be."

"Why should I be in trouble? I had to register for my tutoring school."

"George, I believe that's a story you're making up."

"God, Sinclair, what a thing to say. I don't go around accusing you of being a liar."

He looked at me sort of confused. Then he

said, "Well, it doesn't sound sensible to me."

"Don't give me that jive, Sinclair. If I have to be tutored, I have to be tutored."

"We'll see what my father says."

I didn't have to be told that. I went on up to the porch. Uncle Ned was sitting there, grunting his way through the paper. When he saw me he put the paper down. "Well, George," he said.

"Gee, Uncle Ned, I'm sorry I forgot to tell you about registering. I thought probably Pop told you."

"He never said a word. What's it about?"

"I'm supposed to go to tutoring school this summer. I flunked a lot of stuff."

"I'm surprised. Your father told me you'd done pretty well this year. Not as well as Sinclair, of course, he's an exceptional student, but well for you."

"I guess he was sort of ashamed of me. Maybe that's why he didn't mention about tutoring school."

"What exactly did you fail?"

"American history, and math, and I almost flunked French, too." The minute I said math I knew I'd made a mistake.

"Math? I could have helped you with that. What was the course?"

"Beginning algebra. I guess that's another reason why Pop didn't tell you about it. He knew you'd want to help me with my math, and probably he didn't want to bother you. I mean, being busy the way you are."

"Nonsense, I would have been delighted. With a student as exceptional as Sinclair around, I never get much practice tutoring. Well, all right, now what is this school?"

"I have to go in again on Thursday for some placement tests. Then after that I find out when my classes are."

"And where is this school?"

But I'd been smart enough to work that one out. Being a teacher, Uncle Ned was bound to have books and things in his office where he could check up. "The Hedley School," I said. "It's on East Fifty-eighth Street. Between Park and Lex." It was a pretty classy school in a classy neighborhood, and I picked it so Uncle Ned would believe that I was going to some respectable place, not some dump where I might get mugged. The reason why I knew about it was because this friend of mine, Josh Harris, got sent there the summer before because he'd practically flunked out of school.

"The Hedley School. That's a sensible place."

"Well, I guess that's what Pop figured. That's why he's sending me there."

"And you have to go back to New York on Thursday?"

"Yes, for placements."

"I see," he said. Then he put out a grunt. "I think it must be time to wash up for supper, George."

I was pretty glad to get away and I went. But I knew that he was going to do two things.

The first thing would be to write Pop an air-mail letter in Paris asking about it; and the second thing would be to call the Hedley School. I wasn't exactly sure what I was going to do about the second thing, but I had the first thing figured out. So after dinner, when Sinclair was in his room working out some chess problems from a book he had, I went onto the porch where Uncle Ned and Aunt Cynthia were sitting and said. "Have you got Pop's address written down somewhere? I'm supposed to write him a letter."

"It's in that little red book by the telephone, George," Aunt Cynthia said. I went out into the hall where the phone was, found the little book, and took it upstairs. I shoved it in my pocket, borrowed a piece of paper and a pencil from Sinclair, went into the bathroom and locked the door. Then I opened the book. I figured that they'd have written Pop's Paris address in pencil—people don't usually put in temporary addresses in pen, especially people like Uncle Ned, who's got everything carefully figured out. It wouldn't be sensible, putting in temporary addresses in pen. And I was right—the address was in pencil—Hotel Le Mazarin, 63 Rue St. André des Arts, Paris 6, France. It also had the phone number—325-32-51. I copied the address and phone number onto the piece of paper I'd borrowed from Sinclair, folded that up and stuck it in my back pocket. Then I carefully erased the name of the hotel and tried to think up another hotel name that sounded French. The only French name that came to my mind was Gaston; so I put down Hotel Gaston, 20 Rue St. André des Arts. Then I changed the phone number a little. After that I went into Sinclair's room, where I was staying, wrote Pop a nice letter about how Sinclair wasn't so bad after all, we were having a lot of fun working on his computer, sealed up the letter, and took the address book back down to the telephone table where it belonged. So that was that. Of course, if I got into a car crash and was killed, Uncle Ned wouldn't be able to write Pop about it, but I figured that was just as well—it'd spoil his vacation to have his only son killed in a car crash.

CHAPTER SIX

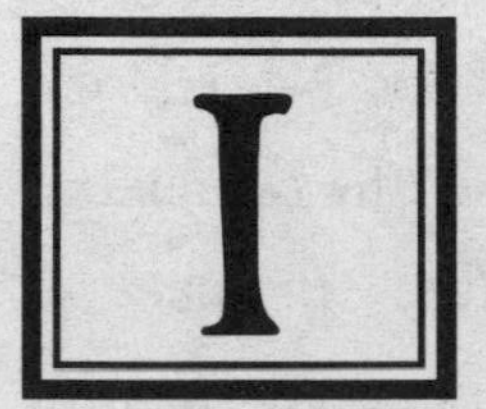

I DON'T SUPPOSE you've ever been through something like this. I guess most people haven't, but at the beginning there's such a swirl of things happening to you that you don't have much time to think. There always seems to be five people around you telling you what to do, and you just go numbly from one thing to the next, obeying orders. I guess when you finally get rich and famous you stop obeying orders and give them out instead, but at the beginning they want you to do what you're told. It's pretty confusing, because a lot of times they don't bother to tell you why, they just give you an order.

On Thursday Woody kept me busy getting

ready for this conference with Mr. Fenderbase, and I didn't have time to think about it. From the way Woody talked about him, I figured he must be a close friend of God's. Mr. Fenderbase was going to settle my fate. If he liked me, I would be George Stable, The Boy Next Door, and get to be rich and famous. If he didn't like me I would be George Stable, prisoner at Sinclair State Pen. In order to get ready for this conference with the friend of God's, Woody took me out to some stores and bought me a lot of Boy Next Door clothes. According to Woody, Boys Next Door wear brush denims and purple and green shirts. He bought me about six different outfits. Man, was it expensive. The shirts cost fifty dollars each and shoes seventy-five dollars, and like that. Most of the things I never did see the price of—they just added everything up and Woody paid it with his credit card without batting an eyelash.

Then the next thing was the haircut. I don't mean a regular haircut like the kind Pop gets me that costs two fifty. I mean, a razor cut that cost thirty-five dollars and took almost two hours. Man, I went crazy sitting in that barber's chair. For boredom, it was worse than watching Sinclair build his computer. Then, when they finally got me all jazzed up in these fancy clothes, they took me over to this photographer to have my picture taken.

That was pretty funny, or it would have been if everyone hadn't been so serious about it. In order to give me a Boy Next Door look, they'd rigged up about six feet of porch railing. I was supposed to lounge around on this playing the guitar and eating an apple. I pointed out to them that you couldn't hold an apple when you're playing the guitar unless you held it in your teeth, which was going to look pretty silly. They didn't care much about that, they got me leaning against the railing, with the guitar sort of propped up against me, and the apple in my hand. There was supposed to be a big bite gone out of the apple so it would look like I was really eating it. I had a lot of trouble taking a bite that would satisfy the photographer. First, the bites weren't big enough, and then they were too scraggly and not neat enough. The photographer kept saying, "Give us a nice clean bite, sonny, give it a touch of class." Finally, when I'd bitten up nearly a whole bag of apples he cut a bite into one with his jackknife. I doubt if I could have made a bite that big if I'd had a mouth like a horse, but it satisfied the photographer.

Between the photographs and the clothes and the haircut, there wasn't much time to talk about music. But Woody told me not to worry about it, he and Superman were giving it a mull, and would come up with something. "We've got to firm up your image before we can decide how the music is going to go. Superman wants to give it the Nashville sound, but I'm not so sure. I think I'd rather get into something with a heavier background—oboes and strings, maybe. I've got a feeling for not going too heavy on the hick stuff. We'll be stuck with it if the country music boom collapses. Myself, I don't like the hayseed image, I see you more as a suburban Boy Next Door—you know, the newspaper route and hanging out at the pizza parlor, playing the jukebox. It's good identification—those suburban kids are the ones who have the money to spend on records, anyway."

"I hope we're going to make the record soon," I said. "I'm beginning to get nervous about it."

"Don't worry, baby. Woody's got it all in hand."

I'd been around the music business long enough to know how these things work. You don't just go into a recording studio and sing a few songs and come out again. There's a whole huge deal involved. It might take weeks to make one record. Generally they have the backup group come in and record first. Then when that's on tape, the singer comes in and works against the recorded background. They might even do it in three or four stages—the rhythm section first, then the strings if it's that kind of record, and then the choral group, and finally the singer, all on separate tracks. The advantage of doing it this way is that they can balance it all in the studio later. Also if they want to change something in the background, say, they can just fix up that part without having to bring everybody else back to record the whole thing over again. I must say, it doesn't seem like a very natural way of doing things. I would sing my part in an empty studio with the background being fed into my ears with earphones. It's hard to do that, because you can't hear what you're singing very well. You get out of tune a lot. I must say the whole thing made me feel more like a soldier in the army than an artist. But that's the way you get rich and famous in the music business.

In the afternoon, Woody took me to a meeting with Superman. "He wants to have another look at you."

"I wish he'd stop treating me like a poodle in a dog show."

Woody shrugged. "He's a cold-blooded guy, baby. He doesn't think of his artists as human beings. He sees them as so much clay he can peddle if he can mold it right. As far as he's concerned, George Stable isn't a boy, he's a hunk of meat with sales potential. Sure, it's cold-blooded. But it works—he's got more gold records to his credit than nearly anybody in the business."

"I still don't like it. He makes me feel creepy."

"You don't have to like it," Woody says. "You just have to go along, and by and by you'll be rich."

When we got to Superman's office, he was sitting behind his desk wearing that Camelot T-shirt. He stared at us. "I just wanted to see if you guys were still alive," he said. "How's it going?"

"Good," Woody said. "We've got some test shots made, and we're beginning to move on the music."

"Hmm," Superman said. "Fenderbase wants to go over the situation soon. Don't leave any loose ends." He leaned back in his chair, lit one of his big cigars, and began blowing smoke all over us. "George, if we're going to work together, we ought to get to know each other better. Why don't you come around to my place some evening and we'll have a chat?"

The last thing I wanted to do was go around to Superman's place for a chat. He scared me. "Gee, maybe it would be best after Pop gets back from Europe. I'm supposed to be up at my Uncle Ned's in time for dinner at night."

He nodded. "We'll work it out sometime. If I gave Uncle Ned a bell, he'd understand."

I didn't want that either, but I didn't say anything, and Superman didn't say anything either, and we left.

So that was that. Woody told me to be in New York on Monday, and I took the train back to Pawling. I was getting pretty used to riding that train. One good thing about it was that it only took ten minutes to walk from the station to their house. I got there in time for supper. When I got there Uncle Ned was sitting on the porch, grunting away as usual. "How did it go, George?" he asked.

"Okay, I guess," I said. "I start on Monday."

"How often do you go down?"

"Monday, Wednesday, and Friday. For now, I mean. They said they might have to change that as we went along."

"I see," he said. "I guess it's time to wash up."

That's all he said about it, and it made me suspicious. I figured he got some letters out on the subject, and was playing cool until he got some answers. But I didn't know that for sure.

Sinclair wasn't so good at keeping his cool, though. After dinner, we were up in his room, playing chess. Being beaten at chess by Sinclair wasn't my idea of fun, but I felt sort of guilty about what I was doing, so I agreed to play to be nice. The first game he beat me in about six moves with some trick he'd learned. The second game I concentrated more, but he still beat me in fifteen minutes. "Let's quit," I said. "It must be pretty boring for you to beat me so easy."

"It isn't much of a challenge, George. You ought to concentrate more."

"I can't," I said. "I don't have that kind of mind. I mean, if I was more of the concentrating type, I wouldn't have flunked so many courses."

He gave me a look. "George, I don't believe you flunked any courses. I believe you made this whole thing up. You're not going to tutoring school. You're doing something else."

It just went to show that Sinclair wasn't as dumb as he seemed. "Sinclair, don't be crazy," I said. "Why would I go to all the trouble of going into New York everyday if I didn't have to?"

"I don't know," he said. "But I'm suspicious."

"Don't be crazy, Sinclair. If your father believes me, why shouldn't you believe me?"

"That's what you think. He doesn't believe you."

"How do you know that, Sinclair?"

"I heard him talking to my mother."

"What do you mean you heard them?"

"I just heard them."

"You were listening."

He blushed. It was the first time I'd ever caught him doing something wrong. "Well, anyway, what did they say?"

"I'm not going to tell you," he said.

"What kind of crap is that, Sinclair?"

"Oh, well," he said, "I'll tell you. My father said it didn't make any sense. Why would your father send you up here if you were supposed to go to summer school? Why couldn't you have stayed with some friend in New York?"

"I would have, Sinclair, but Stanky was going to music camp and his parents were going to California."

"Is that the only friend you have?"

"No, I have lots of friends."

"And I suppose they were all going to music camp."

"I don't want to talk about it anymore, Sinclair. I don't care if you don't believe me, it's true anyway." I got up from the chess table. "I'm going to read," I said. And so that ended the conversation; but I knew I had better do some practicing on my lies—they weren't good enough.

CHAPTER SEVEN

On Monday I took the train down to New York again. The train ride was beginning to get boring. There wasn't anything very spectacular about the sights along the way—just trees and roads with cars humming along them faster than the train, and closer into the city, a lot of buildings, about half of them slums. On top of it, there was something wrong with the tracks, so the train bounced and jounced so much that sometimes you couldn't even read, you just had to sit there being bumped around and wishing they would fix whatever was wrong. So when the tracks were bouncy, I'd look out the window at the trees and when they were smooth, I'd read some S-F, but still, it was boring, and I was always glad to get into New York. There are a lot of things wrong with New York, but at least it isn't boring.

But on that Monday it wasn't very exciting, either. For one thing, it was drizzling. For another thing, the meeting I was supposed to come in for had been canceled. "I would have called you, babe," Woody said, "but I don't have your phone number, remember?"

"Oh," I said. "I forgot. I'll bring it in next time."

"I'd have thought you'd have learned it by this time."

"I guess I should have," I said. "I have trouble memorizing phone numbers sometimes."

"Bear it in mind, babe. But be here on Wednesday. We're meeting with Fenderbase and the biggies."

So there I was stuck in New York. I couldn't go back up to Pawling, because I was supposed to be in tutoring school. Oh, I suppose I could have said that classes were canceled for some reason, or there'd been a fire in the boiler room, but I didn't want to add any more lies to the ones I'd already told: I was having trouble enough keeping them straight already.

I decided to go down to Greenwich Village. I figured I might run into somebody I knew. There was always a chance that some friend of mine would be shooting baskets at the West Fourth Street courts, if it wasn't drizzling too hard. Anyway, it would feel kind of good to be back in my own neighborhood for a few hours. I could go to Crespino's, which is a lunch counter Pop sent me to a lot when he was too lazy to cook, and have a hamburger. It would make me feel at home. So I walked over to Times Square and took the Seventh Avenue local down to Sheridan Square, and then just by habit I started walking down West Fourth Street, just sort of idling along, and all at once I found myself standing in front of my own building. Our apartment is in the front, on the fourth floor. I crossed over to the opposite side of the street and looked up. There were some lights on in the living room. I didn't know who Pop had rented it to, whether it was some single person or a family, although a little apartment like ours wouldn't hold a very big family. Of course, with these sublets, sometimes they cram in more people than usual. I mean, it might be some professor from New York University, which was only a couple of blocks away on Washington Square, and maybe he had his wife and his kid there, too. I'll admit it, I was getting pretty curious. I mean, suppose some kid was sleeping in my bed, where I'd slept all my life, and doing his rock collection or enameling kit or whatever his thing was, on my desk. It gave me a kind of funny feeling to think about that, as if I had a sort of twin, like in that doppelganger movie where this guy had a double who was just like him, only in another world. I wondered if he was using any of my stuff. When I'd gone up to Sinclair's I'd taken pretty near all of my clothes, mainly because I didn't have very many, and my acoustic guitar, and some of my records, because I knew Sinclair didn't have any rock, and my bathing suit and stuff like that. But most of my junk was still in the apartment. I mean, like my camera and light meter, from the time when I had a hobby of photography. It was a secondhand Nikkormat that Stanky sold me for twenty-five dollars, which was a pretty cheap price, mostly because he wanted somebody to do his photography with. I didn't last at it very long. For a while Stanky and I went around taking shots of addicts nodding out in doorways and the Empire State Building through fire escapes and stuff like that which was supposed to be artistic. But then came having to develop them and print them in this darkroom Stanky had rigged up in the basement of his building. That was pretty boring, and I gave up photography as a hobby. Stanky was disgusted with me, but I explained to him that I didn't have much stick-to-itiveness. He said, "I know that, but you have to get over it, George." I said, "I don't think I ever will." He said, "You ought to try," and I said, "Sorry about that," and that was the end of the photography. But I still had the camera and the light meter and some other darkroom stuff, and I wondered if whoever was living there was fooling around with it. It would make me sore if he was, even if I never used it anymore.

And all of a sudden I decided to go on up and see. It made me kind of nervous. I knew that Pop wouldn't want me bothering the people who were subletting. He'd say that they were paying good money for the privilege of living there, and we didn't have any right to come barging in. But I decided to do it anyway, I'd say I was somebody else. I had my own key, so I let myself in the front door, climbed up the stairs to the fourth floor, and knocked on our door. I waited for a minute, and finally a woman's voice said, "Who is it?"

"It's George Scampi," I said. The Scampis lived just below us, only they didn't have any George; their children were all grown up, Agnes Scampi used to baby-sit me when I was a little kid.

"Scampi?"

"I live downstairs."

She opened the door a crack and looked out.

"I didn't mean to bother you," I said, "but there's some water leaking down. It might be from your radiator. It happens a lot."

"Oh," she said. "Well, come on in." She opened the door up. She was around twenty-two or something, and she was wearing blue jeans and a T-shirt which was smeared up with paint.

I walked in. "They're always having leaks up here," I said. "Sometimes it's from the radiators, sometimes it's from the toilet or the sink. You never can tell where it's coming from."

"Well, have a look around," she said. She had some drawing paper tacked onto Pop's drawing table, and she was doing some kind of watercolor sketch, but from where I was standing I couldn't see what. She went back to the drawing table, but she didn't work. Instead, she sort of watched me. I went into my bedroom. The bed wasn't made, and there was a lot of women's underwear flung all over the place. It made me kind of sore to see my room all messed up—I mean, I didn't keep it so neat myself, but at least it was my mess. I fooled around in there for a minute, and then I went into the bathroom and pretended to look at the sink pipes. It was kind of funny to see a lot of lady's pills and stuff in there instead of our toothbrushes and Pop's razor and shaving cream and all that. So then I checked the kitchen, which had strange foods in it, too, and finally I went back into the living room.

"Well, I can't find anything," I said. "I guess it must have stopped by itself."

"Stopped by itself?"

"Yeah, it does that sometimes."

"Well, okay," she said.

But I didn't want to go. I was still curious to find out if anybody else was living there. I mean, maybe her husband was at work and her kid was riding his bike in Washington Square. Besides, I didn't have anything else to do. "I guess you're a painter," I said.

"After a fashion," she said.

She wanted me to go, I could tell that, so she could get back to her painting. "I'm kind of interested in painting," I said. "I take art in school." I walked over to her picture, and then suddenly I saw something out of the corner of my eye that stopped me. It was my little teddy bear key chain. It was hanging from one of the knobs on the swivel lamp Pop had over his drawing table, just sort of dangling down over the table. It made me feel kind of creepy to see it hanging there, I mean, considering that it was my special thing and didn't have anything to do with her. So I blurted out, "I see you have a teddy bear key chain."

"What? Oh, that."

"The kid who lives here has one like that."

"It's his, I imagine," she said. "It's sort of cute."

There wasn't anything more I could say about it. If I'd admitted who I was in the first place, maybe I'd have been able to say it was my lucky charm or something, and she'd let me take it, but it was too late for that. "Well," I said, finally, "I guess I'd better go. Maybe I'll see you again."

"Fine," she said. "Although I usually don't like being interrupted when I'm working."

So I left; there was nothing else to do. I checked out the West Fourth Street courts, but it was still drizzling too much for basketball, so I went over to Crespino's and ate a hamburger and a milk shake, and then I killed some time up on Eighth Street in the record stores; and finally it was time to go up to Grand Central and take the train back to Pawling. What a boring day. And to make it worse, halfway up to

Pawling on the train I finished my Heinlein book and had nothing to do but stare out the window at a lot of wet trees.

Of course every time I got back to Sinclair's I was faced with a new worry—had Uncle Ned caught onto something? He didn't say anything when I came in, except his usual "I guess it's time to wash up for dinner," and he didn't say anything about it at dinner—we just carried on a conversation about Isaac Newton's theory and how it was different from Einstein's theory of relativity. Uncle Ned didn't believe in wasting the dinner time with a few jokes or some interesting story about what happened that day, the way Pop and I did, which I guess is one reason why Pop never spent much time up there. Uncle Ned's idea was that you were committing a sin unless you launched right into some lively topic like Isaac Newton or air pollution. I wasn't in favor of air pollution, mind you, but I didn't see why we had to have it along with our pot roast every night. But to be honest, so long as he didn't bring up anything about my summer school I wasn't going to be too upset, even if the conversation wasn't much more fun than looking at wet leaves for an hour.

But as it turned out, he was only playing it cool. After dinner, when I was sitting out on the porch reading, so as to escape from being beaten at chess by Sinclair, which I would have to have done if I'd hung around his room, he came up and sat down next to me. "Well, tell me, George," he said. "How's your school going?"

"Pretty good," I said. "I mean, it's just at the beginning, it's sort of confusing."

"I suppose so. What exactly are you taking?"

He was trying to trap me, that was clear. "French and math. They didn't have enough for American history or I would have taken that, too."

"That sounds like enough," he said. "It isn't sensible to try to do too much at once. I suppose they've really loaded you down with homework."

"I guess they will," I said. "Only we haven't got our books yet."

"That seems like bad management. Perhaps if you told me the name of the books I could get them for you."

I was beginning to sweat around my eyebrows. "Well, they said they'd have them next time."

"I see. You mean Wednesday—day after tomorrow."

"That's what they *said*—but maybe something will go wrong."

He stood up. "Let's hope not, George." Then he went into the house.

CHAPTER EIGHT

RIDING DOWN TO New York on the train I thought about it. Why was everybody so against me being rich and famous? It just didn't seem fair. Especially when it probably wasn't going to work out anyway. I mean, what difference did it make to Pop if I went down to New York and fooled around Camelot Records, instead of sitting up in Uncle Ned's barn watching Sinclair solder wires onto his computer? Or why should it matter to Uncle Ned what I did? He wasn't my father, and besides he had a perfect son. He should have been satisfied with that instead of meddling around with me. There wasn't any way he could make me perfect, no matter what he did. It wasn't any use for him to try.

But there wasn't much point in trying to figure out why he was against my being rich and famous; because I knew perfectly well that as soon as he found out what was going on, he'd capture me away from Camelot Records and keep me locked up in Sinclair State Pen until Pop got home. And that wouldn't be any help, either, because as soon as Pop found out that I'd been sneaking off to New York to be rich and famous he'd hit the ceiling, ground me for four or five years, and cut off my allowance for the rest of my life, too. I didn't know how long it would take for Uncle Ned to get the idea. I was positive he'd written Pop, and the only question was how long it would be before his letter would come back marked "No Such Hotel" or however the French would say it.

But there wasn't anything I could do about that but pray, so I turned my attention to another trouble, which was the big conference I was going to that morning with Mr.

Fenderbase, the close friend of God's. I wondered what he was like. Even Superman was scared of him, and Superman was a pretty scary guy. I mean, having been in jail and all.

The way Woody made it sound, this conference was the biggest event of the year, bigger than the World Series or the President's State of the Union address. Naturally, Superman would be there and Woody and a couple of guys from the publicity department and the music director and most important of all, Mr. Fenderbase, the president of Camelot Records. "This is it, baby," Woody had told me. "They'll decide whether it's go or no go. You got to be sharp. When Superman says to bop a little, bop."

When I got up to the Camelot offices, the receptionist told me to go down to the conference room. There was a long table in the middle of it. Everybody's place was set with a pencil, a pad of paper, a glass of water, and an ashtray, as if we were about to sit down to some kind of dinner. Woody was already there when I got there, pacing around the room and nervously smoking. "Where've you been, baby?" he asked.

"What?" I said. "I'm five minutes early."

"Well, let's be on time next time," he said.

He was too nervous to realize what he was saying, and I admit I was getting pretty nervous myself. I wanted to sit down, but I didn't know where my place was. I began to pace around at the other end of the room from where Woody was pacing, and then the door opened and a man came in and said, "Georgie, darling, it's marvelous to see you."

It took me by surprise. He was a guy named Damon Damon whom I'd known from the music business before. Damon Damon was a musical director. In the music business they like to have one guy out of every twenty or thirty who knows something about music, and Damon Damon was it. He really did know about music—chords and notes and how to breathe when you're singing and stuff like that. He was sort of nutty, but everybody liked him because he knew what he was talking about and wasn't full of crap like everybody else. People used to call him Damon Damon the Button King because he always had extra buttons on the cuffs of his jacket. Also, he wore these amazing vests that had fancy buttons on them, too.

"What are you doing here, Damon?" I said.

"Didn't anyone tell you, darling? I'm musical director of Camelot. I'm going to be in charge of your career if they decide you're going to have one." He unbuttoned his jacket and held it open to show me his vest, which was red with big yellow flowers on it. "What do you think of my waistcoat, sweetie? Absolutely delicious, isn't it?"

I must say I was glad to see Damon Damon. He was somebody I could trust, even if he was nuts. He didn't worry about where he was supposed to sit, but plopped into a chair and then patted the one next to it. "Here, Georgie, come sit by me and tell me how much you admire my waistcoat."

So I sat down next to him; and just then some other people arrived and plopped down, and then finally Superman came in on his aluminum crutches with another guy, who turned out to be Mr. Fenderbase, the relative of God's who was president of Camelot. He had a lot of distinguished gray hair and a distinguished fake suntan he'd got at his health club and he was wearing a distinguished gray suit that went well with his fake suntan. He gave me a firm handshake and looked me straight in the eye, the way people in the music business do when they're trying to give you the impression that they're sincere. In the music business you can always tell a liar by his firm handshake and the way he looks you straight in the eye.

So everybody milled around for a few minutes and then Mr. Fenderbase said, "All right, Superman, where do we stand?" His voice was soft and distinguished like his gray hair and his suntan.

"Got a good clean concept here, Mr.

Fenderbase. George Stable, The Boy Next Door. A kid who's no musical genius, just a red-cheeked, barefoot down-home kid of the kind every American mother wishes she had for a son instead of the slump-shouldered yahoo she's got. Woody, tell George to stand up so Mr. Fenderbase can get a look at him."

"Stand up, George, so Mr. Fenderbase can get a look at you."

I stood up and stared at Mr. Fenderbase in a sincere way so he'd know I was as big a liar as he was, and then Mr. Fenderbase waved his hand and Superman said, "Woody, tell the kid he can sit down."

"You can sit down, George," Woody said, and I sat down.

Mr. Fenderbase put his hands behind his head and stared at the ceiling. "Why are we selling records to America's mothers, Superman?"

"Acceptance in the home, Mr. Fenderbase. That's the big concept today. You take your average fourteen-year-old girl, anything Mom likes, forget it. She's rebellious, she doesn't want to *know* from Mom. But now your ten-year-old, she's still involved with Mom, she'll go along with Mom's ideas. And Mom is going to think that George Stable, The Boy Next Door, is a doll. She's going to say to herself, 'That's the kind of cute little sucker I want my Mary to go around with when she's older.' He's a good kid, he's that polite newsboy who brings the paper to the door instead of heaving it into the hedge, he's the kid at the supermarket who carries your bag out to the car just to be nice. He's the boy Mom wants for her daughter instead of a weirdo like that friend of her son's she keeps turning up under the newspapers when she vacuums the television room. Who needs him, with his scraggly beard and his dirty jeans? All she has to do is just *think* about that one laying a finger on her little Mary and she has to push home half a box of Librium to stop shuddering. What we've got for her is George

Stable, The Boy Next Door. And once we sell Mom, she'll sell little Mary and we're golden."

Mr. Fenderbase went on staring at the ceiling. "Why are we selling records to ten-year-old girls, Superman?" he said in his soft, distinguished voice.

"The name of the game is moola, Mr. Fenderbase. M-o-o-l-a. The big dollar. There's a honey of a buck in this and nobody's got his fingers into the hive yet. According to market surveys, the average American ten-year-old girl has discretionary income of over one hundred dollars a year—allowance, baby-sitting money, the birthday fiver she gets because granny is too lazy to buy a present. It all adds up. There's five million girls out there in that nine-to-eleven group, with half a billion dollars to spend every year. And they're going to blow it all on dairy freezes and training bras if we don't get to them first."

Mr. Fenderbase went on staring at the ceiling, and everybody sat there waiting for him to give out his next pronouncement. Finally, in that low distinguished voice, he said, "What about the boys?"

"Right on target, Mr. Fenderbase," Superman said. "They've got lawn-mowing jobs and they're throwing away even more money on dairy freezes than the girls. They'll sit there in front of the TV watching George Stable, The Boy Next Door do his number and they'll be drooling all over their Boy Next Door T-shirts wishing it was them up there. Oh, we're not going to get them all, of course. Some of them are going to be jealous of The Boy Next Door and go around telling everybody that George Stable is a custard-face, but the hell with those little soreheads, who needs them? In our concept, the male audience is a bonus."

Superman stopped talking. Everybody looked at Mr. Fenderbase again, who was still sitting with his hands behind his head, staring at the ceiling. We all sat there waiting, and finally he got his head down from the ceiling, looked around the room, and said, "I like the concept." Everybody breathed a sigh of relief. "But do we have the right boy?"

I guess Superman figured he'd got over the worst of it, because he took out one of his big cigars, lit it, and began blowing smoke all over everybody except Mr. Fenderbase. "That's what we're here for today. Is George Stable The Boy Next Door? Let's find out. You're on, Woody."

Damon Damon gave me a tiny wink and then Woody said, "I'll tell you one thing, folks, Boys Next Door don't grow on trees. A good clean-cut kid who projects wholesome freshness and still doesn't fall over his feet in front of a microphone is almost a freak these days. I've been working with this boy for three years now, and I can tell you he's for real, the genuine article. Straight as a die, honest as the day is long."

"Frankly," Mr. Fenderbase said in his soft, distinguished voice, "I prefer a boy with a little larceny in his soul. It's hard to cheat an honest Boy Next Door."

That was supposed to be a joke, so everybody began roaring with laughter, slapping the table with their hands, and half passing out in their chairs. Woody roared right along with the rest of them. Finally, the uproar calmed down and Woody said, "But I don't want to give you the idea that this is some half-baked innocent who's going to have a hot flash every time somebody speaks to him. He's been in show business for six years already—in the chorus of the Westport Watch Hour when he was eight, one of the beavers on Captain Windy's Laughboat for two seasons until his voice broke, a couple of television specials—there aren't many kids around with that kind of background, folks."

It was all lies, except for that one television special I was on once for six seconds. I hadn't any background in the music business, folks. I was just an ordinary kid who'd studied singing a little and guitar a little, who happened by luck to be on television for six seconds or whatever it was. As for not stumbling over my feet or getting hot flashes when I got in front of a microphone, why I was just as likely to stumble over my feet or get a hot flash as anybody else. Everything Woody had said was just plain lies, and it made me disgusted with him. But being my agent, he figured it was his job to tell lies. It seemed right to him. An agent was supposed to make his client look good and since the other agents were lying about their clients, Woody figured he had to lie about his, too.

But I didn't like it. It made me feel uncomfortable. In the first place I didn't like being talked about like a poodle in a dog show. They could at least admit that I could understand English and knew what they were saying. In the second place, suppose Mr. Fenderbase or Superman got to asking me a lot of questions about the Westport Watch Hour or the Laughboat? I wouldn't have the right answers and in about a minute they'd know it was all made up and either I'd have to tell them that Woody was a liar, which I wouldn't want to do, or take the blame myself, which I wouldn't want to do, either.

But what I didn't like about it most of all was being a phony. I'll admit, I'm not against lying on principle. I mean, I guess I lie to Pop almost every day—you know, little stuff like did I finish my homework before I went over to Stanky's or did I sweep under my bed. That kind of lying isn't phony; it's just to keep your parents from running your life all the time. A kid who didn't lie to his parents sometimes wouldn't be normal.

But all this stuff—Woody's lies about my marvelous background and Superman's whole long thing about the mothers of America falling in love with me, and all those girls spending their baby-sitting money on my records—well, it was just plain phony, that's all there was to it.

And then the question was: Would I give

up a chance to be rich and famous just to avoid being phony? Would anybody? Would that be stupid? I didn't know; but I didn't have any chance to decide right then, because all of a sudden Mr. Fenderbase said, "Superman, have the boy bop a little." So Superman turned and said, "Woody, have George bop a little for Mr. Fenderbase." And Woody said, "George, bop a little for Mr. Fenderbase."

There they were treating me like a poodle again. I knew I was supposed to come on with something like, "Gee, Mr. Fenderbase, I'm just an ordinary kid and what a big thrill it must be for me to be in the same room with somebody who is a close relative of God's." And I tried to say it. But try as I might, I just couldn't get the words out through my teeth. The right words were going around in my head; all I had to do was open my mouth and say them. But I just couldn't get my mouth open. I couldn't sit there staring around, though; I had to say something. So I blurted out, "I don't want to make a big deal out of it, Mr. Fenderbase, but since I'm right here in the room with you, why don't you ask me your questions instead of asking Woody or Superman or somebody else?"

They all stared at me. Out of the corner of my eye I noticed Damon Damon give me another wink. That encouraged me, and I decided the heck with it, if they wanted to make somebody else The Boy Next Door, that was okay, I'd just as soon go back to Sinclair State Pen as be a complete phony all the time. So I said, "I realize that you all know a lot more about the music business than I do, but since it's my life that's going to be messed up, I think I ought to have some say in it."

Then I stopped and sat there. They stared at me some more, waiting to hear what Mr. Fenderbase said before they opened their mouths. He put his hands behind his distinguished gray hair and stared at the ceiling for a while. Then he began to whistle. Finally he said, "That's straightforward enough, George.

I'm glad to discover that you're not just a stuffed doll." He tore his eyes away from the ceiling and looked around the room at everybody, drumming on the table. Then he said, "All right, Superman, let's get on with it."

He stood and everybody else stood and there was a hubbub all around the room. Woody put his arm around my shoulder and gave me a squeeze. Damon Damon the Button King winked at me, and finally, when Fenderbase had got himself hubbubed out of the room, Superman himself came over on his crutches and patted my shoulder, which made me sore. "Woody, get him up to publicity and see what kind of a concept the boys can work up." Then he said, "George, come on down to the office with me. I want to talk to you for a minute."

He turned and began to swing himself out of the room on his crutches, and I followed along behind him. The truth is, I didn't like him. I guess it wasn't fair not to like him, him being a cripple and all, but there was something about him that struck me wrong—that completely bald head and those popped-out blue eyes without any eyebrows. I just didn't want to have very much to do with him.

We got to his office and he swung down into the chair behind his desk. He didn't ask me to sit down. I stood in front of the desk. Out the window behind him I could see a tiny airplane coming in to land at LaGuardia Airport.

He lit a cigar and blew smoke all over me, staring at me out of those blue eyes. I waited. He took the cigar out of his mouth and rolled it a bit in his fingers. Then he said, "George, do you use drugs?"

"No."

"Never?"

"No."

"I think we'd better get this straight, George. If The Boy Next Door gets busted for drugs, he isn't The Boy Next Door anymore. The Moms of America aren't going to buy a Boy

Next Door who's stoned half the time, right?"

"Right."

"Now get this in your head. Camelot Records is about to sink a quarter of a million dollars into George Stable, and that's just to get the balloon off the ground. We aren't going to blow that kind of money just because you want to turn on some Saturday night. From now on, you're the cleanest-living kid in America. Right?"

I didn't like being bossed around like that, but he scared me. He was tough, that was for sure, and I was afraid to cross him. "Right." I said.

"Okay," he said. "There's honey money in this for you as well as us, George. Keep it in mind. You can end up a millionaire if you handle yourself right. Got it? You start working with Damon Damon on Monday. I want to cut the demo record within a week. And if that goes, we're off and running." I started to turn to go, and then he said, "Oh yeah, I haven't forgotten about getting you up to my place for a chat one of these days. We'll have to schedule that soon."

CHAPTER NINE

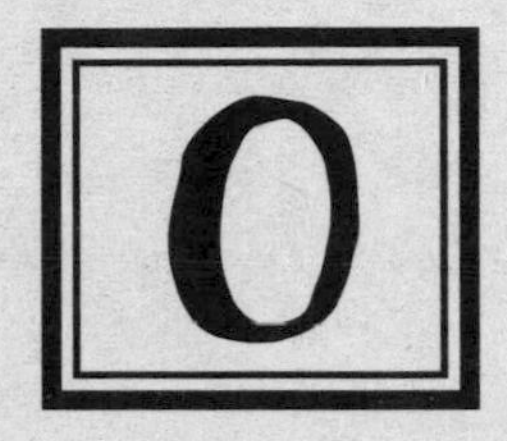

F COURSE THE meeting only took an hour, and there I was, with about three hours to kill. I wished I'd told Uncle Ned that the hours for the tutoring school were earlier, but if I'd done that the meeting would have gone on all day, and Uncle Ned would have wanted to have known why I was late for dinner. Not that I was in any rush to get back to sit around admiring Sinclair's perfectness; but in New York I didn't have any place to be, I just had to hang around. I went over to Sam Goody's on Third Avenue, which isn't too far from Grand Central, and looked at records for a while, and then I decided to go down to the Village again, to see if I could get into a game on the West Fourth Street courts. But nobody I knew was playing, so I watched for a while, and then I just sort of stood there, trying to decide what to do next. And I was standing there, when I saw the woman who was subletting our apartment come down West Fourth Street onto Sixth Avenue, and go into the liquor store.

I was kind of sore at her. I knew it was unfair, she couldn't help it if she sublet our apartment, and I guess if she was paying for it she was entitled to mess it up if she wanted. The thing that bothered me most was my little teddy bear key chain. I had a funny feeling about that, her just sort of taking it over the way she had. I mean, it didn't bother me she was using our towels or our plates and forks and stuff, but that teddy bear key chain was my special thing, it was mine, and I didn't want anybody else having it for their thing, even though it didn't really hurt me anyway. I'll admit it, I didn't pay a lot of attention to it when I was home. I didn't carry it around, or put my own house keys on it, because it was too big to have in my pocket all the time. But even if I ignored it a lot, it was still mine, and I didn't like her messing with it.

And all of a sudden I realized that I could easily go upstairs and get it. I had my keys with me. It wouldn't be any problem at all. Of course there was no telling how long she'd be gone. She might be gone for the rest of the day, or she might be coming right back from the liquor store. But it would only take me about two minutes to get up to the fourth floor, and another minute to grab the key chain and get out again. Even if I met her when I was coming back down the stairs she wouldn't think anything of it. I was supposed to be George Scampi, I belonged in the building.

She still hadn't come out of the liquor store. I crossed Sixth Avenue and trotted up West Fourth to our apartment, and looked around again. She wasn't in sight. Quickly I opened the front door, and began to run up the stairs. I'd done that often enough. When I reached our door I unlocked it, and dashed into the room. I didn't bother to shut the door, because I was going right out again.

But I didn't go right out again, because the teddy bear key chain wasn't hanging on Pop's lamp anymore. It was gone. I stood there, thinking. Maybe she'd put it back in the bedroom. I ran in there and looked, but it wasn't on the bureau. I pulled open a couple of drawers, but it wasn't there either. I went into the kitchen to see if she'd put it there. And suddenly from behind me came her voice saying, "Okay kid, don't move."

I turned slowly around. She was standing there holding Pop's palette knife out toward me. "Hey," I said.

"I mean, it," she said. "If you move, I'll run you through."

I began to sweat and get red. "Listen, I can explain."

"I guess you'd better," she said. "You might begin by explaining what you were doing around here yesterday."

"Honest, there was a leak—"

"The heck there was. I went down to the Scampis last night to see if everything was okay and they told me there wasn't any leak, and there wasn't any George Scampi, either."

"Oh," I said. I really felt like a complete fool. "Well, I can explain anyway. I'm George Stable. This is our apartment."

She blinked. "George Stable? Sam Stable's son?"

"Yes," I said.

"Why should I believe that? I think I'd better just call the cops."

"No, no," I said.

"So tell me the truth, then."

"It's the truth. I'm George Stable. See, look, here's my subway pass." I took out my wallet and showed her my pass.

"How do I know you didn't steal this?"

"There are some pictures of me in my bedroom. In the bottom drawer. My friend took them. He has a hobby of photography."

She stared at me. Then she said, "You hold it right there, kid." She backed up, keeping her eyes on me all the time, and backed into my bedroom. In a minute she returned with a pile of pictures that Stanky had taken of me. She looked at them and then she looked at me, and finally she said, "Well, it's you all right. So you're Sam Stable's son. What are you doing, haunting the place?"

I didn't know what to say. I'd told so many people so many different stories I hardly knew what the truth was anymore. "I'll be honest," I said. "I got sort of homesick to see the old place."

"Homesick? You've only been away from here two weeks."

"Well, I know," I said. "I guess I was sort of curious to know who was living here."

"Well, you found that out before. What did you come back for today?"

I got red and hot. "Well, I wanted my key chain."

"Key chain?"

"With the teddy bear on it." It seemed kind of silly to go to all this trouble for a key chain.

She took it out of her pocket. It had her keys on it. "You mean this?"

"It's sort of a good luck charm for me."

She laughed. "You mean you were willing to risk a breaking-and-entering charge just to get this?"

"I didn't think of it that way." I said. "It's our apartment, you can't get arrested for breaking into your own apartment, can you?"

"You sure can, kid, when I'm subletting it. Don't forget it." She took her keys off it and handed it to me. "Here," she said. "And don't break in anymore."

"Thanks," I said.

"I knew Sam Stable had a kid, but I didn't think you'd be as screwy as he is."

"Do you know Pop?"

"Sure. I'm doing some work for Smash Comics. That's how we met. I used to be a great fan of *Garbage Man* when I was a kid. I thought it was terrific when mild-mannered advertising executive Rick Martin turned into a garbage man and burned holes in things with his smell."

She seemed pretty nice after all. "Do you draw a comic strip?"

"I'm doing some coloring." I knew about that: the main artist usually draws the pictures in pen and ink and then they have some lesser ones to put in the colors. "I thought it was terrific the first time I got to color *Garbage Man*."

"How come you decided to sublet our apartment?"

"The lease on my old place ran out, and I took this to give me time to find another place. It's pretty tough finding places—your pop will be back in two more weeks and I still haven't got anything."

"Maybe you can live with us for a while."

"I don't think Denise would like it."

"I guess not," I said. Although I couldn't think why not.

"Listen, George," she said, "I've got some work to do. But if you feel homesick again, stop by if you like."

"Thanks," I said. And I left.

Uncle Ned didn't say anything to me about school that night. It was beginning to worry me. I'd been up at Sinclair's for about two weeks, and it had already been ten days since he'd written Pop a letter about me. It seemed to me that the letter should be coming back any day now, and then what would I do? My big hope was to sweat it out for two more weeks. I didn't figure that Pop would come out to Pawling to get me—he'd just call up and ask how things were and tell me to come home on the train. And hopefully Uncle Ned wouldn't bring up anything about the tutoring school. But maybe he would; there were a lot of worries in the whole thing, but all I could do was tell myself not to worry about them.

Anyway, I didn't have much time for worrying. George Stable, The Boy Next Door, was on fire at Camelot. We were getting ready to cut the test records, and there were meetings and conferences going on all the time. A lot of it was just a big waste of time. Woody would tell me to be somewhere at ten and I'd get there a quarter of ten just to be on the safe side, and then Woody would show up at ten-fifteen. We'd sit around until nearly eleven and by that time somebody would have changed his plans and we were supposed to come back after lunch. After a while I got the idea and brought along a S-F book to read. And a couple of times I went down to our old apartment and talked to the woman who was subletting it. Her name was Barbara Feinberg. She was pretty nice; she didn't seem to mind it when I came down and talked to her.

But even when the meetings got going, a lot of times they didn't seem to be about anything: people would say things like, "We haven't got a clean concept here," and, "I'd like to know what the distribs feel about it, let's get a slant from Smithers at Retail Outlets," none of which I could understand. Finally they'd all decide to "give it a mull" and "keep on truckin'" and the meeting would break up.

Even when the meetings were actually about something, they hardly ever had anything to do with music. Most of the time they had to do with publicity and my image and what kind of a haircut a Boy Next Door should have. Take for example the meeting with the publicity guys. There were two of them—a tall, skinny guy who looked as if he were going to cry, and a short, round one who seemed happier. They didn't even bother covering up that they were being phony. They just made stuff up left and right as if it was a perfectly normal thing to do. "Where ya' from, George?" the short, round one said.

"West Fourth Street," I said.

"No, you're not from West Fourth Street.

You're from someplace in the country," the skinny one said.

"Got any relatives in some hick town somewhere?" the round one said.

"I'm staying with my cousin in Pawling. That's upstate."

"What kind of a place is that?" the round one said.

"Just a small town," I said. "There are a lot of farms there."

"Pawling?" the skinny one said, looking worried. "Is there really such a place? It's important that you come from a real place. Sometimes they send fan mail to the hometown and it looks bad when it comes back marked, 'No Such Place.'"

"It's real," I said. "I've been there."

"Naturally you've been there," the round one said. "It's your hometown. Any cows and like that? Real country-time?"

"My cousin has a barn, only there aren't any cows in it. They use it for cars."

"Barns," the skinny one said. "That sings, barns are good."

"What about a main street?" the round one said. "We may have to put on a homecoming parade—George Stable, The Boy Next Door returns triumphantly to the something little town where as a schoolboy he something, something, while imbibing the something something that has made him world famous. Some crap like that."

"Maybe we ought to wait until he gets world famous before we plan any parades," the skinny one said, looking worried again.

I wondered what Sinclair would think of me parading down the main street of his own hometown. I figured he'd commit suicide. "There's a regular main street there," I said. "Drugstores and banks and the railroad station."

"Let's hear it for Main Street," the round one said.

"That railroad station might sing," the skinny one said. "What else? What kind of things did you do when you were a kid up there? Ice skating? Sneaking apples out of Farmer Brown's orchard? Pitching maple syrup or whatever the hell they do?"

"Well, the thing is, I didn't actually live there, so I couldn't—"

"Now, George," the skinny one said. "Let's not confuse the issue. Pawlville is your—"

"Pawling."

"Pawling is your hometown, so naturally you must have lived there. I can see you playing baseball in cow pastures, or sledding down Farmer Brown's barn, your cheeks red and a colorful scarf flying along behind you."

"You don't sled down barns, dummy," the round one said.

"Don't be picky. I can see you roasting corn on sticks over an open fire, and putting the hens to roost every night to earn money for your first guitar."

I began to giggle.

"Don't giggle," the skinny one said. "This is

serious. I get paid twenty-two thousand dollars a year to do this. All right, what about a family? You need a family. What's your mother like?"

"She's dead. She died a long time ago."

"She won't work out, then, will she?" the round one said. "What about your old man? Maybe if he was dead too, we could sell you as an orphan—that's always good for a tug at the heartstrings. Growing up with your mean aunt who took away your guitar so you had to sneak out into the woodshed and practice at night."

"George Stable, The Orphan Next Door doesn't sing," the skinny one said.

"Anyway, my father's alive," I said.

"Too bad," the round one said. "That eliminates the orphan bit, anyway. What's he do, your old man?"

"He's a comic strip artist. He draws *Frankens-Teen*."

"Too sophisticated," the skinny one said, worriedly. "We can't possibly have that. He'd better be a dentist."

"Dentists make too much dough," the round one said. "How about he's a street cleaner? Do they have street cleaners up there in Pawling?"

"I don't think so," I said.

"They must have street cleaners," the skinny one said. "Otherwise how do they keep the streets clean?"

"Come on, dummy," the round one said. "The Boy Scouts clean it up. Right, George?"

"I don't really know," I said. "I guess they don't throw so much stuff around as we do here in New York."

"That's a fair bet," the skinny one said.

"Boy Scouts," the round one said. "Hmm. Maybe his old man is the Pawling scoutmaster."

"That's fairly tasty," the skinny one said. "Let's put some butter on it."

"Won't the real scoutmaster get sore?" I asked.

"Naw," the round one said. "We give him an autographed record if he promises to keep his mouth shut."

That was the way it went. In the end they made Pop a carpenter, because carpenters reflect the sturdy, independent qualities for which country people are famous. They gave me a regular mother, and invented a whole lot of stuff about pitching hay and roasting apples. By the end of it, I wasn't George Stable anymore, I was somebody else. So was Pop: I wondered what he was going to say about being a carpenter in Pawling.

The publicity conferences were only a part of it. There were conferences on my clothes and conferences on whether I ought to work in nightclubs or just in concerts and conferences on how the records would be promoted and a lot of other things. Superman was at a lot of these conferences, and a couple of times he brought up about that chat we were supposed to have over at his apartment. I kept stalling. I didn't have any reason for stalling; I mean, he wasn't going to hurt me or anything. I just didn't like being around him too much, with his blue egg-eyes always staring and those huge strong arms and shoulders he got from walking on crutches all his life. But it was hard to keep stalling. And one day, as we were coming out of a conference he said, "Hey, Georgie, what about dropping by my place tomorrow afternoon around six?"

I blushed. "Gee, I can't Superman," I said. "Uncle Ned is taking us all to a drive-in that night."

"Okay," he said. He stared at me with those blue egg eyes. "What about next week?"

There wasn't much of a way to get out of it. "Well, I guess that would be all right," I said. "Only I have to check with Uncle Ned first."

"It's a deal, then," he said. As far as I was concerned, though, it wasn't a deal. I figured I could easily work up some excuse about how Uncle Ned was taking us to Danbury to the fair or something.

They were finally beginning to worry about my songs. They'd picked two or three that I thought I might do, and they'd ordered some more from songwriters, and after that I started working with Damon Damon on the music. It wasn't as much fun as sitting around listening to guys make stuff up, but I was glad to do it because at least it was real.

Besides, I liked Damon Damon. He was kind of flaky, but he was serious about music and he made me work pretty hard. One day in the rehearsal studio he said, "Of course, they won't use any of these songs—they'll throw them out and get different ones—but we may as well work on them, it will give us something to do. I consider this whole business one of the more insane episodes in what has admittedly been a reasonably ludicrous life, but at least you will be able to sing properly. What do you think of my waistcoat? It's super, isn't it?"

I wasn't feeling much like working. "Yeah, it's nice," I said.

"One redeeming feature of the music business is that you can dress as you like."

"That's probably true," I said. "But you

know what worries me is all this phoniness. I mean, making up all that stuff about my hometown, and spending all this time trying to figure out what kind of a haircut a boy next door has. It's pretty phony."

He nodded. "Quite true, dear boy," he said. "You may as well face it, this isn't art, this is commercial music. You're a nice boy, George, but let's be honest, there are thousands of kids your age in the United States who can sing and play the guitar a little. The difference between the ones who get their pictures on album covers and the ones who stay in Swamp Valley, Kentucky, is packaging. The people inside the packages are pretty nearly interchangeable. Of course, you need somebody with a little musical talent, but basically what Superman looks for is somebody who's pleasant-looking, intelligent enough to understand what's required of him, and willing to take orders without making too much of a fuss. Oh, he doesn't want a sheep, of course. He wants somebody with some sort of spark that will communicate to audiences. But he most emphatically doesn't want some kid arguing with him all the time about his art."

Hearing all this made me feel lousy. "You mean I really am a poodle in a dog show?"

"Oh, it's not as bad as that, Georgie. I mean, after all, you stand to gain a great deal by going along with Superman. He knows what he's doing, mind you, dear boy. He is a very shrewd cookie indeed. And just suppose by some miracle you happen to hit big. You sweat out a few years, then you get yourself a high-priced lawyer to get you out of your contract with Camelot, and you make a deal for yourself that'll make you rich for life."

"It certainly makes me feel lousy to hear you say this," I said.

He shrugged. "Nobody's forcing you, Georgie. It's a question of paying the price."

"Why do you bother staying in the music business, then?"

"Goodness, dear boy, everybody in the business isn't like Sup—isn't a gangster. It may come as a shock, but there are lots of perfectly nice people in it. To be sure, there are absolute flotillas of sharks about, ready to eat you up if they get a chance, but you'd be quite surprised at the number of people in the business who actually care about music. Some of them are quite fond of it, really."

"Do you like being in the music business, Damon?"

"One learns to take the bitter with the sweet, dear boy. I know it's absurd, but I enjoy puttering around with music. After a while you get to know who the gangsters are and you keep clear of them as much as possible."

"Listen, Damon," I said, "I heard Superman was in jail for drugs once."

"Oh yes, it's a perfectly fascinating story. He was part of a huge drug ring, absolute millions of dollars involved, but they never were able to pin anything very important on him. I think he only did three years or so. It was quite a scandal in the music business, I assure you."

"How come he got his job back?"

"Oh, he didn't get the same job back, dear boy. But he came out of jail a reformed character, and gradually he got back into the business."

"What exactly did he do?"

"Apparently he murdered somebody, George, but they couldn't prove it. Gives you that prickly feeling, doesn't it, to know that we're working for a murderer."

CHAPTER TEN

WHEN I GOT home that night, Uncle Ned was sitting on the porch reading his newspaper. On the porch table beside him was a letter, and I knew right away what it was, because it was one of those blue airmail letters with the red stripes along the edge. As I came up onto the porch he folded his newspaper neatly, laid it carefully on the table, and picked up the letter. "Oh, George," he said.

"Hello, Uncle Ned," I said, trying to be as polite as I could.

"George, I'm worried about something. I wrote your father a letter a while ago and it's been returned. Apparently I had the address wrong. You don't remember the name of the hotel your father was staying in, do you?"

I scratched my head. "Gee, Uncle Ned, I don't."

He stared at me. "You've written him, haven't you? I thought I remember you doing that."

"I wrote him a couple of times," I said.

"I was sure you had." He paused for a minute. "It's curious that my letter should be returned and none of yours were."

It wasn't curious to me, though, it was just my usual dumbness. How could I have been so stupid? "Well, gee, Uncle Ned," I sort of stammered out, "I don't know. I mean, I have his address written down somewhere in one of my notebooks. Maybe the French post office made a mistake."

"Let's see what your address book says."

Slowly I went upstairs and into Sinclair's room. He was sitting at his desk working out some math problems. He stopped when I came in. "Boy, are you in trouble, George. What did you do?"

"None of your business, Sinclair," I said.

"My father said, 'Sinclair, George has been lying to us about his activities. I hope you haven't been involved.' Naturally, I told him I wouldn't lie to my own family, 'You only hurt yourself when you do that.'"

"Go jump up and bite your tail, Sinclair." I found the piece of paper with Pop's address written on it, and slowly I went back downstairs and out onto the porch. Uncle Ned took the piece of paper. Then from his pocket he took out the address book that sat by the telephone. He opened the book, and compared the addresses. "Quite different, aren't they, George."

"Gee," I said, scratching my head. "I wonder how that could have happened?"

"If you look closely you can see that somebody erased the old address and put in a new one."

I scratched my head, but I didn't say anything

more, just stood there feeling hot and red and beginning to sweat.

"George, I'm not even going to ask you what you've been doing these past three weeks. Your father will be home in a week and he can deal with it. All I can say is that I'm terribly disappointed in your behavior. It is not something we normally encounter in this family. I believe Sinclair said to me himself, 'You only hurt yourself when you deceive people.' I'm going to ask you not to leave the house or the grounds until your father comes for you. If you can't be trusted like an adult, George, you'll have to be kept home like a baby."

I went up to Sinclair's room and lay down on my bed.

"What did he say?" Sinclair said. "What kind of punishment did he give you."

"Shut up, Sinclair, or I'll beat the crap out of you."

They told me I could come down for supper, but I didn't feel like seeing any of them, so I read for a while and then I went to bed.

The next day everybody treated me as if I were sick or dying or something. I mean, I was in real disgrace. Aunt Cynthia and Uncle Ned spoke to me in low voices, just stuff like "Please pass the butter," but you'd think they were pronouncing the death sentence on me from their tone of voice. The way they were carrying on you'd think that nobody in the family had ever lied to anyone before. You'd have thought I'd been responsible for starting a typhoid epidemic or making a big crack in the world.

Sinclair wasn't so gloomy about it, though. He was just plain curious. He'd never done anything bad in his whole life and it seemed to him that I was pretty unique. It was pretty interesting to him to actually be able to associate with a criminal, although we weren't doing much associating. I didn't have any reason to be polite anymore, so that morning when he asked me to help him with his computer I told him to get stuffed. I thought he would go away and leave me alone when I said that, but instead he just hung around, begging me to tell him what I had done wrong. But I wouldn't give him the satisfaction. He could ask his father if he was so damn curious.

By lunch time I was getting pretty fed up with it all. Uncle Ned took Sinclair off waterskiing, but he didn't ask me to go. I knew he was doing it just to teach me a lesson—he hadn't taken us waterskiing for a week. It made me sore, but there wasn't anything I could do about it. So I went up into Sinclair's room and read. I'll admit it, I had an inclination to mess up Sinclair's room—really mess it up, heave all of his chess sets around and throw his clothes on the floor and so forth, but I didn't. I just lay there for around a half an hour, and then I heard Aunt Cynthia's car start up and go down the driveway.

I was alone. I lay there for a while trying to think of what I could do to get even with everybody. I couldn't think of anything, though, except to start smashing stuff. I would have liked to have done that, but I didn't have the guts. I didn't see how I could last out there for another week and I knew it was going to be worse when Pop got home. He'd really give it to me for everything I'd done, like trying to be rich and famous, but at least Pop wouldn't treat me like I'd caused the death of some saint. He'd rant and rave and ground me until I was practically ninety, but about a week later he'd forget about it and we'd go back to normal. Of course, if I was still trying to be rich and famous, the whole thing would be pretty hard to forget about. I wondered what Pop was going to do about that?

Or what was *I* going to do about that? I was supposed to be in New York for some conference the next day. What could I do, just call up Woody and tell him to forget about the whole thing, Uncle Ned had grounded me and they'd have to get another Boy Next Door? And then about three months later I'd see this other Boy

Next Door on television being rich and famous, and I'd just have to sit there being jealous. I thought about that for a minute, and suddenly I realized that I couldn't take any of this stuff anymore. I got up and searched around in Sinclair's closet until I found my suitcase. I quickly flung all of my clothes into it that I could find. A lot of them were missing. I figured that Aunt Cynthia had some of them in the laundry. Then I shoved a couple of S-F books into the suitcase, and took off out of the house and down to the railroad station. I didn't go right to the station, though. There was about an hour until the next train into New York, and I knew that Uncle Ned and Sinclair might come home from waterskiing. Once they realized that I was gone, they'd go right to the railroad station looking for me. So I went over to the next street and kind of hung around there until I heard the train whistle blowing. Then I ran back to the station, keeping a sharp lookout for Uncle Ned's car. He wasn't around, and I figured he was still waterskiing. The train pulled in and I jumped on. And two hours later I was in New York.

There was only one place to go—down to our own place in Greenwich Village. I didn't know if Barbara Feinberg would let me stay there. Probably she wouldn't. But I had a good reason for going there, which was, if Uncle Ned called the cops, he couldn't say I was running away from home, because I was home. So I went down there and knocked on the door and Barbara let me in. "What's up, kid?" she said.

I took a deep breath. "Barbara, I just ran away. I need someplace to stay."

"Ran away?"

"Yeah, I got into trouble with Uncle Ned. I can't stand staying there anymore."

She sort of sighed. "Well, come in." I came in and put my suitcase down. "How about a Coke?" she said.

"Thanks," I said.

She got me the Coke and I sat down on Pop's daybed and drank it.

"So tell me what happened."

"Nothing," I said. "I mean, they got on my back about something."

"That's nothing new, George. Grown-ups are always getting on kids' backs about things."

"Yeah, well I can't stand it anymore."

She lit a cigarette and stared at me for a moment. Then she said, "Look, it isn't any of my business, but my advice is to go back. Just pick up your suitcase and go back. Running away from home isn't as groovy as it sounds. I know. I did it."

"You're doing okay."

"For a long time I wasn't. I ran away because my parents wouldn't send me to art school. They wanted me to go to some fancy college they'd picked out. Was that dumb. I could have studied art at the college, but now look at me, I'm working nights as a waitress at some cockroach restaurant in order to pay for art school and I'm about four years behind everybody else."

"Why didn't you go home before?"

She shrugged. "I don't know, after a while it gets to be too late for things. I was sixteen when I took off and came here. Of course I was scared to death for about a month, and then I began to meet some people, and after a while I started living with this guy, and it all seemed pretty groovy for a couple of years. But then he got busted for drugs, and they nearly nailed me too, and I began to get another look at the thing and wonder where I was going and where I'd be in another ten years. And I started thinking about art school."

"Why didn't you go home then?"

"By this time they weren't speaking to me, I couldn't go home. I mean, maybe I could have if I'd come crawling back and kissed their feet, but I wasn't about to do that."

"Where are you from?" I asked.

"Some little place in Ohio you never heard of. That's another part of the trouble, every-body out there knew I'd run off and was living in a pad in Greenwich Village. Naturally that was a big disgrace and it made it hard for my parents to forgive me for disgracing them."

"You don't even write them letters?"

"I do now. In the past couple of years I got straight with them, more or less. My old man came to New York about a year ago and we talked about it. I call them up about once a month, or whenever somebody has a birthday or something. So let me tell you, Georgie, I know what I'm talking about."

"But your life is more interesting than just going to college," I said.

"The hell it is. Waitressing in a cockroach restaurant isn't more interesting than anything. Take my word for it, Georgie. Go home. Tell your Uncle Ned you've learned your lesson and go home."

She lit a cigarette and I looked at her. Finally I said, "There's a reason why I can't go home. I'm supposed to be in New York getting rich and famous." And I told her the whole story—about Pop and Denise going to Europe and Sinclair's computer and Woody and Superman and Mr. Fenderbase and all the rest of it. And she stared at me and smoked and shook her head at the interesting parts. Finally, when I got finished, she said, "Are you standing there telling me that you're on the verge of being a millionaire?"

I got kind of embarrassed. "Well, I don't know if it would be that much."

"You're serious? This whole story is true?"

"Yes," I said.

"Wow. How'd you like to be my boyfriend, George?"

I grinned. She was kidding, but I was glad she liked me. "Sure," I said.

"Well, listen, we can't fool around with money like that. You better move in with me for a few days until we can figure out what to do."

So that's what I did. And the next day I went up to Camelot to work with Damon Damon. They were going to make the test record in a couple of days. The song they had settled on was pretty silly. They had had it specially written. It was some crap about a girl who was in love with the boy next door, and at the end of the song it turned out, naturally that I was the boy next door. The melody wasn't too bad, nothing special, but not too bad. It was the words that were awful. But Superman said it was right, and Damon Damon agreed. "Of course, the lyrics are simply beyond belief, dear boy, but it's commercial."

And we were working about on this song, "The Boy Next Door," when Woody came in with these two public relations guys, the tall, sad one and the short, round one.

"Hold up a minute, Damon," Woody said. "We got a little something we want to work out." He turned to me. "Georgie, we want to go up to this hometown of yours and do a little shooting."

"We've got to get some crap organized for the fan magazines," the round one said.

"Right," said the tall, skinny one who looked as if he were going to cry. "Some photographs of The Boy Next Door at his house next door. This cousin of yours—he'll let us use his house for background, right?"

"Sinclair?" I croaked out.

"Sinclair?" the round one said. "That's the name of a gas company. What does he think he is, a gas station?"

"Dummy, the Sinclair Gas Company went out of business when Lincoln was president."

"It's an old family name," I said. "From Uncle Ned's family."

"Uncle Ned?" The round one slapped his thigh. "That's beautiful, that's real down-home time."

"It sings," the skinny one said. "It couldn't be better if I'd made it up myself."

I was thinking fast. "Well, gee, I think they've gone away. They go up to Maine fishing a lot. I mean, for vacation. So I guess that won't work out."

"Sure it will," the round one said. "Better not to have them hanging around anyway. They'll just get underfoot asking for your autograph."

I began to really worry. "Well, see I guess I should explain, the reason why they went up to Maine was because they had a fire there at the house. It burned the whole porch and part of the kitchen, and there are carpenters all over the place now."

The skinny one shrugged. "We don't care about the house, all we need is the barn—a few shots of you pitching the horses or whatever they do."

"That's what I was going to say," I said. "The fire started in the barn."

"Why does this always happen to me?" the skinny one said.

"Because you're a high school dropout, dummy," the round one said. "If you'd finished high school, you could have been a big-time executive like Woodward. Come on, Woody, what's the story?"

Woody sighed. "Now, George," he said patiently, "I know you've been under a lot of pressure, but this isn't any big deal. These guys are pros, they'll go up there with you. They'll find the backgrounds they need. Just relax and do what they tell you. We want to do it in a couple of days."

"Well, gee—"

Woody put up his hand. "Please don't argue with me, George. We've got to get some stuff going for the fan magazines. You want to be in the fan magazines, don't you? *Vocal Star Magazine*, *Teen Hits*, those ones."

The skinny one nodded. "Modest, unassuming George Stable, The Boy Next Door, still does his share of chores around the home, despite his newfound fame. In the picture at left, he shovels the hay out of his father's barn. At right, helping Mom wash the dishes."

"That's going to be a little hard to take a picture of," I said, "seeing as she's been dead for thirteen years."

"All right, Aunt whatever her name is," the round one said. "Uncle Ned has a wife, doesn't he?"

"Aunt Cynthia."

The skinny one shook his head. "We'll have to change that. 'Aunt Cynthia' doesn't sing. There isn't an editor in New York who can spell Cynthia correctly. What's the simplest name you can think of?"

"Bob," the round one said.

"Aunt Bob? In this picture George Stable, The Boy Next Door, helps his Aunt Bob wash the dishes. It doesn't sing."

"Cut it out, you clowns," Woody said. "George, be ready to go up there tomorrow."

CHAPTER ELEVEN

HAT WAS I going to do about it? I couldn't tell Woody the truth—he'd get upset and start having long phone conversations with Pop, and if that was going to happen I might as well commit suicide right in the beginning. Somehow, I was going to have to avoid going to Uncle Ned's. Maybe I could pick out some other old abandoned barn along the way and say it was Uncle Ned's. Or some house where nobody was home or something. Otherwise, all I could do was pray.

I thought about it all day, and I was still thinking about it at five o'clock when Superman suddenly heaved himself into the studio where I was rehearsing with Damon Damon. "Hold it a minute, Damon," he said. We stopped playing. "Georgie, I think it's time we had our chat," Superman said. "I've got a lot of things I want to go over with you. Come on by my apartment this evening—around seven o'clock."

"Well, gee," I said. But I couldn't think of anything, so I said, "Okay." He gave me the address, which was some posh place up in the East Seventies, and left.

"What's that all about?" Damon asked. "Superman never struck me as the type for little chats. Is he serving tea?"

"Oh, I don't know," I said. "He keeps saying he wants to get to know me better."

"How odd," Damon Damon said. "It hardly seems Superman's thing, having little chats with thirteen-year-olds."

"Have you ever been to his place, Damon?"

"I've never been asked, dear boy. I don't think that Superman and I have much in common."

"I guess not," I said. "I wonder what he wants to talk about?"

"I wouldn't bring up the subject of murder if I were you," Damon said. "I presume he's a bit sensitive about it."

I didn't want to go; he scared me too much. I mean, what were we going to talk about? But when I got up there I was kind of glad I'd come. He had the fanciest apartment I'd ever seen. I mean, the Stankys have a pretty fancy place, in this brownstone on Eleventh Street, but it was one of these sort of old-fashioned places with a lot of antique furniture. Superman's place was brand-new, with everything modern. There were these great big windows in the living room, so you could sit there and look down on the East River, with the Fifty-ninth Street Bridge and then down further the Williamsburg Bridge and the Brooklyn Bridge. You could see way out into Brooklyn and Queens, and up north to the Triboro Bridge, too. There were wall-to-wall carpets everywhere, and a fireplace, and this modern glass and aluminum furniture. Boy, was it fancy.

Some other guy let me in. I didn't know whether he was Superman's butler or a friend of his or what. But he showed me into the living room where Superman was sitting in a big modern chair. He brought Superman a drink and me a Coke, and then he left. I decided he was some kind of servant, because he didn't hang around with us, but went away someplace.

There was a record player going, kind of softly. "Do you just play Camelot records?" I asked, to be polite.

He laughed. "Georgie, I listen to enough of that garbage all day long. I mostly listen to jazz when I'm at home. Or Baroque music. Vivaldi."

"My Pop likes Vivaldi," I said. "He keeps trying to get me to like it, too, but somehow I just can't. I mean, it doesn't turn me on or anything."

"Is your Pop still in Europe?"

I didn't like to think about Pop coming home too much. "He's supposed to come back at the end of the week," I said.

"I guess you'll be glad to see him," he said.

"I guess so," I said.

So then he began asking me a lot of questions—what grade I was in, and how I did in school, and about my friends, and my hobbies and a lot of stuff like that. It wasn't what I'd call a chat—more of a quiz, if you want to know. But I didn't much care. It was kind of nice sitting in that fancy apartment looking out at the East River and all those bridges, drinking a Coke out of a fancy glass with ice in it, instead of right out of the can the way I usually did. And I began to decide that maybe Superman wasn't so scary after all. He was just one of those people who seem scary.

Finally Superman said, "Well, I guess we've both got things to do."

So I finished off my Coke, put down my glass, and got up. "Well, thanks for the Coke," I said.

"That's okay, George," he said. "See you tomorrow." The servant sort of popped out from nowhere, and started to show me toward the door. But then Superman suddenly said, "Oh listen, Georgie, maybe you can do me a favor?"

I stopped. "Emmett, hand me that package from the sideboard in the dining room." The man went out and in a minute he came back with a square package wrapped up in brown paper. It was tied up with string, and there was Scotch tape on it too. "George, these are some tapes of your backup group. I want the arranger to have a listen to them. Be a good guy and drop them off. It isn't far out of your way to Grand Central."

I took the package. It seemed to have five or six boxes of tape in it. There was an address on them, somewhere on East Thirty-sixth Street.

"All right," I said. I didn't tell Superman that I wasn't going to Grand Central, but down to Greenwich Village.

"Be careful with them, George. They're the only copies we've got."

I said I would be, and I left. I took the Lexington Avenue subway down to Thirty-third Street, went over to the address on the package, and rang the bell. But nobody answered. I thought that was kind of funny: I figured Superman would have made sure that the guy was home before he'd send me over with something as valuable as the tapes. For a moment I thought about leaving them with the super, but then I decided I'd better not if they were that valuable. The only other thing to do was to take them back to Superman's, or to take them home. I didn't really want to see Superman anymore. The easiest thing would be to take them home. I could go up to the arranger's house in the morning with them, and if he still wasn't home I could take them up to

Camelot and give them back to Superman.

So I went home. Barbara Feinberg was eating some canned hash for supper. "Where've you been?" she asked.

"I was up at Superman's. He wanted to have a chat."

"Do you want something to eat?"

"I'm pretty hungry, I could make myself a sandwich," I said, hoping that she'd cook me something instead. I put the tapes down on the table.

"There's some more hash in the pan," she said. "I'm not going to eat it all." Then she pointed at the package with her fork. "What's that?"

"Tapes of my backup group. I was supposed to deliver them to the arranger, but he wasn't home."

"What do they sound like?"

"I don't know," I said. I went out into the kitchen and looked into the frying pan. There didn't seem to be an awful lot of hash in it. I guess Barbara Feinberg didn't know how much kids eat. "Listen, how much of this hash are you going to eat?"

"You can finish it up. I'm full."

I got down a plate and scooped the hash onto it. Then I got four pieces of bread out of the icebox, smeared them up with butter and peanut butter, poured out a big glass of milk, and carried it all out to the table.

"Good Lord," she said. "Peanut butter and hash?"

"I don't mind it," I said.

"It's your stomach." She leaned back and lit a cigarette. "So what does your backup group sound like? Is it country or what?"

"I don't know."

"Aren't you curious?"

"Yeah," I said, "I'd like to know if it's going to be a country sound or what."

"Let's play them. That tape recorder of your pop's works, doesn't it?"

"Yeah, it works," I said, shoving a lot of bread and peanut butter into my mouth.

"Well, all right," she said.

"The thing is, I don't know if I should open them."

"How would Superman know?"

"There's Scotch tape on the paper."

"I can get that off," she said, "with turpentine."

"So it wouldn't show?"

"Sure," she said. "There's nothing to it."

I took a mouthful of hash and thought about it. I was pretty curious. "Well, if you think it won't show," I said.

"Don't worry," she said. She slid the package over in front of her, and began unknotting the twine, picking at it carefully with her fingernails until it came loose. Then she took the string off the package and set it aside. Next she went over to Pop's taboret, and poured out some turpentine from her painting stuff into a little bowl. She took a sharp knife, dipped it into the turpentine and slowly, a bit at a time, worked the knife point under the Scotch tape. Rapidly the turpentine dissolved the stickiness on the tape, and it came loose just the way a postage stamp soaks off in water. She went on carefully working the knife under the tape, dipping it back into the turpentine every few seconds, and in about two minutes she had the Scotch tape peeled off. She set the piece of tape aside to dry. Then she unwrapped the brown paper. It was splotched up with turpentine. She set it aside to dry, too. "That smell will disappear after a while," she said.

It was six boxes of tape. "That's a lot of tape," I said. "We can't listen to it all."

She picked up the top box and looked it over. There was no writing on it at all. "Maybe it says something on the reel," she said. She laid the box on the table and lifted the cover off.

But there was no reel of tape inside. Instead

there were a lot of little plastic bags, each filled with whitish powder.

"My God," she said.

"What is it, Barbara?" But without being told, I already knew, and a cold chill went up my back and across the top of my head.

"My God," she said. She lifted out one of the plastic bags, unfolded the top, and sniffed inside. "Cocaine," she said. "You're sitting on a fortune."

"How much is it worth?"

She shrugged. "All I can do is guess. I'd say you might have a kilo of the stuff here, more or less."

"A kilogram?"

"Yeah," she said, "about two pounds. It's probably worth twenty-five thousand dollars, maybe more. That's wholesale. By the time it reaches the street, it'll be worth a hell of a lot more—maybe a quarter of a million dollars."

I gulped. "A quarter of a million dollars?"

"I don't know exactly," she said. "Since my

old boyfriend got busted, I've been out of touch."

She put the tops back on the boxes and stacked them up. Then she began waving the wrapping paper in the air. "We'll give the turps a few minutes to dry," she said.

"Barbara," I said, "the whole thing is crazy. Why would Superman give me the stuff to carry around?"

"Why not?"

"I'm just a kid. I might lose the stuff. I might leave it on the subway or something."

"That's true. On the other hand he probably figured that if he told you it was tapes of your music you'd be pretty careful about it. Anyway, I guess he figured it was a lot safer than carrying the stuff around himself."

"Why?"

She lit up a cigarette and thought about it a minute. "Does this Superman or whatever he calls himself travel abroad a lot?"

"All of these A. and R. guys do. Camelot

has got a couple of English groups under contract, and some Latin bands from Mexico. He goes all over the place to record them."

"That's it, then," she said. "Probably he's acting as some kind of funnel for drugs coming into the country. He's in a good position for it. There have always been a lot of drugs mixed up in the music business; there are always dealers hanging around. So Superman would have contacts here for getting rid of the stuff. The problem would be getting the drugs in—cocaine from Mexico or South America, heroin from Europe."

"Why would he do it? He's got a big job."

"Maybe he's a user himself. Maybe somebody's got something on him and they're blackmailing him, maybe he's just greedy. Who knows? But traveling around like that with a lot of luggage—amplifiers and recording equipment and so forth, he'd have a lot of places to hide drugs. After a while the customs people would get to know him. I mean, he's a big record company executive, who's going to suspect him? So one way or another he gets the stuff in, and then his problem is to move it around New York."

"I can't see why that's a problem, if he's got the stuff disguised as tapes."

She shook her head. "He doesn't want to walk around New York carrying cocaine himself. Suppose his contact gets busted; the narcs stake the place out and there's your buddy Superman walking in with a kilo of cocaine. They'd lock him up and throw away the key. In fact, if he can avoid it, he doesn't even want his contact to know who he is. A lot of times when they nail the contact, they'll let him off with a light sentence if he'll finger the guy above him. So the best thing is for nobody to know who you are."

"But I know. I could finger him."

"Sure," she said. "If you got caught with the stuff, undoubtedly, you would, and Superman knows that. But he'll just deny it. The only way they can get him is if they actually catch him handing the drugs over to you." She took a long pull on her cigarette. "Okay, suppose you get caught making the delivery. So you finger Superman. Now what they have to do is set it up so that there are some undercover agents in the room when Superman gives you the drugs, or at least they're staked out where they can come bursting in at the crucial moment. That isn't going to be easy up there in the Camelot offices. Strangers can't come wandering around without him knowing about it, and you can't very well bring in an undercover guy disguised as your pop—Superman just won't produce the drugs with somebody else around." She shook her head. "It isn't a hundred percent foolproof, nothing is, but it's a lot safer than moving the drugs around himself."

"So I get busted instead of him."

"Georgie," she said, "that is one big problem. We're going to have to do some thinking about that." She stubbed out her cigarette. "I guess the turps is dry. Let's wrap the stuff up."

She wrapped the boxes back in the paper, Scotch-taped them, and tied them up with the twine. Because she was an artist she could do it practically perfectly, with all the creases in the brown wrapping paper exactly in the right places. When she got finished it looked as if it had never been opened.

"That's pretty good," I said.

"I've got good hands," she said. "I should have been a thief. The main question, Georgie," Barbara said, "is what are you going to do about it?"

"I know," I said. "I know that's the main question."

"And there's only one answer. Take that box to the police."

I sighed. "Yeah." I was feeling pretty gloomy. "There goes George Stable, The Boy Next Door."

"It's better than going to jail."

"They don't put kids my age in jail, do they?"

"They sure as heck will do something when they find out you're hauling a kilo of cocaine around New York. Besides, you don't want to be mixed up in this stuff anyway. It isn't healthy work."

To tell the truth, the idea of squealing to the police on Superman scared me a lot. It seemed to me that he was more dangerous than the police. I mean, if the police caught me with the stuff, why I'd explain what had happened, and I didn't think they'd put me in jail. But Superman could do anything; there wasn't any knowing what he would do. Boy, did I ever wish I hadn't got curious about my tapes.

"Barbara, I'm scared of squealing on Superman."

"I can believe that, Georgie. He sounds pretty bad."

"Damon Damon says he probably murdered some guy."

"Murdered somebody?"

"Well, they don't know that for sure.

Damon Damon said they couldn't pin it on him, but during the time that Superman was being busted somebody got killed. Damon Damon says he was stabbed in the back with some kind of pointed thing."

"A knife?"

"That was the funny thing, Damon Damon says it didn't seem to be a knife so much as a sort of spear wound."

"And they think Superman did it?"

"I guess they could never prove it," I said.

She lit a cigarette and sat there thinking for a while. Then she said, "Well look, Georgie, there's one other thing you could do. You could just take the stuff back to Superman tomorrow and tell him the guy you were supposed to deliver it to wasn't home. It's true, isn't it? You weren't lying about that, were you?"

"No, honest, that's true. I rang his bell about six times and nobody answered."

She went on smoking and thinking. "That's funny," she said. "I don't see why he'd have sent the stuff over if he wasn't sure the contact was home." She smoked some more. "Well, listen, Georgie. It's up to you. If it were me, I'd go to the police. But if you decide to just take it back to Superman, I'm not going to squeal on you."

"You think he'll be able to figure out we opened the package?"

She picked it up and looked it over carefully. "No," she said finally. "I did a pretty good job. If you take it back to him and tell him the guy you were supposed to deliver it to wasn't home, he ought to believe you."

"I guess I better think about it," I said.

She got up. "I was planning to go to the movies," she said.

I didn't want to stay there alone with a quarter of a million dollars worth of cocaine. "Is it okay if I go, too?"

She grinned. "As long as you've got your own money, fella."

So we went to the movies. All the way over I kept turning it over in my mind, whether I should go to the police or whether I should just give the stuff back to Superman and forget about it. There were a lot of problems either way. If I went to the police there'd be a big mess, and I figured I was already in enough trouble as it was. I mean, it was likely that Uncle Ned had called the cops to tell them I'd run away; that was just to begin with. And then of course the cops would want to know where Pop was, and they'd call him up in Paris and the next thing I knew he'd be flying home with Denise, good and sore at me for spoiling their vacation. And it'd be the end of The Boy Next Door, that was for sure.

On the other side of it, suppose I took the package back to Superman, and he gave it back to me and just said to take it over to the guy that night. I'd be right back where I started from, only worse off, because I'd know it wasn't tapes I was delivering, but cocaine, and that was illegal for sure. I went on thinking about it all the way over to the Waverly

Theatre and even during the movie it kept popping up, even though it was the Marx Brothers in *The Big Store*. And when we came out of the movies I went back to thinking about it again, although Barbara bought me a peanut butter fudge cone at Baskin and Robbins to take my mind off my troubles. I still hadn't decided anything by the time we got home. I walked up the stairs in front of Barbara thinking about it. My mind was occupied so that at first I didn't realize that the door to the apartment was unlocked when I pushed it open.

But Barbara did. "Georgie," she hissed.

Then I realized, and stepped back. "Didn't we lock it?"

"We sure did," she said. "Get ready to run, they may still be in there."

I stood back, and she kicked the door open. It swung back on its hinges, and there was silence. We stood there waiting. But there were no sounds. "I guess they're gone," she said. "I hope they didn't get my Nikon," she said.

"They probably got your father's high fidelity."

But when we walked in, the high fidelity was there, and so was Barbara's Nikon, sitting on Pop's taboret. There was only one thing missing—the package of cocaine, from the table where we'd left it.

CHAPTER TWELVE

T WAS A GOOD thing I was sleeping in my own bed that night, because if I'd been sleeping anywhere else I wouldn't have slept any all night, whereas in my own bed I was able to sleep some, at least. Oh, how I wished I'd never heard of Camelot Records and The Boy Next Door, and being rich and famous; I wished I was just some ordinary kid who was bored all the time and had nothing to do but wait around until he was grown up. But it was too late for that. The cocaine was gone, and what was I going to tell Superman? I went on thinking about it all night. First, I'd tell myself that Superman would believe me. I'd explain that somebody broke into the apartment and swiped a lot of stuff, and naturally he'd believe me. Thinking that would make me feel a little better, and I'd sort of doze off. And then all of a sudden I'd shoot right up awake again thinking, what if he didn't believe me, he'd probably torture me or something to find out what I'd done with the cocaine. Then I'd tell myself that was crazy, nobody would ever do a thing like that. And after a while I'd get myself calmed down and doze off again; and then something else would cross my mind and I'd shoot awake. It went like that all night, and what with all that stuff going back and forth in my mind, I didn't remember until I actually got up and was eating some eggs that Barbara Feinberg made for me that I was supposed to go up to Sinclair's house that morning and get my picture taken being The Boy Next Door. Suddenly, what a relief. The minute I showed up there Uncle Ned would capture me and turn me over to the police. That would be the end of Superman and The Boy Next Door and all the rest of it.

"Listen, Barbara," I said. "Uncle Ned is

bound to keep me from going back to New York. He'll make me stay there. And Woody'll tell Superman that I was in trouble with my family and couldn't be The Boy Next Door, and Superman won't be able to do anything about it."

"What about the cocaine?"

"I'll just say the guy wasn't at home so I left it by the door. I mean, that's a pretty dumb thing for anybody to do, even a kid, but kids do a lot of dumb things."

"Well, maybe," she said. "He might believe it." She lit a cigarette and leaned over her coffee, thinking about it. "It depends on how crazy he is. If he isn't crazy, he'd probably believe it. There isn't any reason not to."

"Well, that's what I'm going to tell him," I said. "If he ever catches up to me and asks."

"You think your Uncle Ned will keep you from coming back to New York?"

"Oh, God yes. That's his big thing, making sure that everybody is perfect."

By the time I got up to Camelot, I was

feeling a lot better—pretty nervous all right, but not scared completely to pieces. Woody was there with the two public relations guys and a photographer. We milled around for a while, and then we milled down the elevator and got into a Rolls Royce that was waiting out front of the Camelot Building. Woody and the photographer and I got into the backseat, and the two P.R. guys got in front.

I didn't have much of an idea how to get to Pawling but one of the P.R. guys figured it out from a map. Off we went up the West Side Drive. "I've never been in a Rolls before," I said.

"It's for the image," the round P.R. guy said.

"I would have thought The Boy Next Door would have some cheap old car," I said.

"Not your image. Our image," he said.

"I used to have a Rolls once," the skinny one said. "A Rolls-Canardly."

"A Rolls-Canardly? What's that?" I said.

"Rolls down one hill, can hardly get up the next."

"Oh boy," Woody said.

The round one drove and the skinny one sat beside him fooling around with the map. As we went up the West Side Drive away from New York and all my problems, I began to feel a little better. The more I thought about wheeling up to Sinclair's house in the Rolls with the photographer and these other people swarming around me, the better I liked it. It was going to be star time finally, even if it was only going to last for a day. Sinclair and his straight As and his darn computer were going to look like pretty small potatoes. He'd have to stand around and watch me get photographed and envy me and sulk. It served him right for boring me to death.

"Listen," I said. "If I'm the star, how come I have to sit all crowded up in the back?"

"Calm down, George," the skinny one said. "We'll tell you when you're famous."

"Better not mouth off," the fat one said. "He might get lucky and they always take their revenge when they get famous."

"How come I never got famous?" the skinny one said. "I was supposed to be a famous writer, and look at me—a public relations man."

"I had my disappointments, too," the round one said. "I wanted to be a public relations man."

"I thought you were a public relations man," I said.

"He thought he was making a joke," the skinny one said.

Woody sighed. "If you guys are going to keep the wit going all the way up to Pawling, I'm getting off here," he said. "Let's talk about something sensible. Did anybody see the Mets last night?"

So we talked about the Mets, and then everybody began telling music business stories, which are crazy and fascinating and made me laugh. And on we drove in the Rolls Royce, going seventy and eighty miles an hour up the various parkways, and about an hour later we reached the outskirts of Pawling.

Around then I began to get kind of nervous again. What was Uncle Ned going to say when he saw me?

"Where do we go?" the round one asked.

"I'm not sure," I said.

"I thought this was your hometown."

"I haven't lived here much since it got to be my hometown," I said.

"We could ask somebody directions," the skinny one said, "but I'd rather not. The Boy Next Door shouldn't have to ask directions to his own house. It doesn't sing, if you get what I mean."

"I think it's down this way," I said. We made the turn and drove along for a while and soon I began to recognize where I was; and all of a sudden we pulled up to Uncle Ned's house. I got out, walked up onto the porch, opened the front door, and, my heart pounding, shouted, "Anybody home?"

Nobody answered. Where was everybody? I was counting on being recaptured. I walked into the kitchen. "Anybody home?" I shouted again. But still nobody answered. So I went back out the front door. The photographer was taking his equipment out of the trunk of the Rolls and Woody and the P.R. guys were milling around, looking at the house.

"I thought you said the place burned down," the round one said.

"I guess they got it fixed up already," I said.

"That was fast work," Woody said.

"Yeah," I said. "Well, it was coming up to their twentieth wedding anniversary and they had this big party planned, so my uncle hired a lot of extra men to get the job finished in a hurry." I could tell by their faces that they were having a hard time believing that, but they didn't say anything. "My uncle and my aunt aren't at home."

"That's a shame," the skinny one said. "I was looking forward to meeting Aunt Bob."

"Cut that stuff out," the round one said. "You want us to get thrown off the place?"

"I wouldn't mind," the skinny one said.

"I think my cousin might be out back," I said. I started around the house to the back and just as I came around the corner I saw Sinclair coming out of the barn. His eyes were wide open and he was running.

"George," he said. He came up to me. "Boy, are you in trouble." He sounded pretty pleased about it.

"What trouble?"

"My father called the police. They've had an alarm out for you."

That didn't surprise me too much. "I'm surprised," I said. "Listen, Sinclair, where are your parents?"

"Mother is at the library club luncheon. She won't be back for a while. And my father is down at the school—who are all these people?"

I looked around. Woody, the photographer, and the two P.R. guys were coming around the house. "Well, look, Sinclair," I said. "You know how I was going into New York all the time. It was to make a record." So I explained a little bit about George Stable, The Boy Next Door, and how these guys wanted to take pictures of me for a magazine, and Sinclair's eyes got bigger and bigger. Then he began to pout, and just as everybody was gathering around he said, "It sounds like the worst sort of cheap commercial enterprise."

"Oh, it is," the skinny P.R. guy said. "At least we're praying that it will be."

"Cheap, anyway," the round one said. "Let's hope it turns out to be commercial, too. Who's this object?"

"This is my cousin Sinclair," I said.

"Aha," the round one said. "The gas man."

"I told you, the Sinclair Gas Company went out of business years ago."

"He doesn't know it. Give us two dollars worth and where's the men's room?"

"Tell him to clean the windshield and ask him for a map," the skinny one said. "Also the coffee machine doesn't work and does he take Diner's Club cards?"

"Shut up, you guys," Woody said.

I could see that Sinclair was getting pretty sore. Next to being a star and getting in a magazine his perfectness didn't amount to very much. The thing that worried me was that he'd have a tantrum and throw everybody off the place. I didn't mind about that; but I didn't want it to happen until Uncle Ned got home from school and recaptured me. "Listen, Woody," I said, "I've got to talk to you." We walked over to the side. "The thing is," I said, "Sinclair's sore about me being a star and all that. He might try to prevent us from taking pictures. So what I think, it would be a good idea if you could butter him up a little bit."

Woody stared at me. "George, there's more going on here than meets the eye."

"No, no," I said. "It's okay, I just don't want to have a big fight with him."

He frowned at me. Then he said, "Okay," walked back over to the group, and flung his arm over Sinclair's shoulders, which I didn't think was going to please Sinclair very much. "Sinclair, George tells me you're a pretty smart kid, and I wonder if you'd mind helping us out. We want to take some pictures of George around the place and of course since it's your house you ought to be in some of them."

Sinclair looked confused. He kept trying to start the pout across his lips, and he'd get it going all right, but halfway there it would stop and retreat.

Woody took his arm off Sinclair's shoulder and looked down at the ground. "Of course, you might have some objection to having your picture in *Teen Hit* or *Vocal Star*."

That got to him. "Well, I don't know—"

"And then when George gets to be well known, we might need somebody to come down to New York from time to time to advise us. You know a lot more about small-town life than we do. It could be pretty helpful."

"Well, I'd have to think about that—"

"Oh, sure you would. Talk with your

father. It's hard to say how much money would be involved."

That sunk him. "Of course I'm an excellent flute player," he said. "My teacher says I'm the best pupil he's had for years."

"Well, there you are," Woody said. He turned to the P.R. guys. "It's just amazing the way we keep turning up these terrific talents in out-of-the-way places. Isn't it, you guys?"

"I keep fainting from the shock," the round one said.

Woody gave him a look, but it didn't matter because Sinclair was nailed down. "Well, all right," he said, "but I think we ought to hurry before my parents come back. Not that they'd mind me being in a magazine, of course, but it might upset them to have a lot of strangers around." Sinclair was picking up the idea of lying pretty fast.

But of course I was in no rush to get it over with, and I began to think of ways of stalling. The photographer and Woody and the P.R.

guys began walking all over the place as if they owned it, picking out good backgrounds for shots. I sort of lagged along taking my time. They took some shots of me washing the dishes and mowing the lawn and fooling around in the barn and sitting on a pile of logs that Uncle Ned had for the fireplace. Then they took me out front and had me pretend to be polishing the Rolls Royce, except that they shot it from an angle so you wouldn't know it was an expensive car like a Rolls.

By this time of course a crowd of kids had gathered out front of the house, mostly kids from around who were friends of Sinclair's. They stood staring at the Rolls and watching me get photographed. It was star time all right. It felt pretty good and naturally I acted casual and made jokes with the P.R. guys and called Woody "Woody" so that the kids would realize I was pretty important and could call adults by their nicknames. Of course Sinclair tried to put on an act, too, but he didn't know how.

Instead of acting cool and casual, as if he was used to the whole thing, he ran around boasting and saying, "George is a big star and I'm going to play flute in his group, and we're going to be in a magazine," which was very uncool, especially as he wasn't going to be in a magazine.

It went on like this for a couple of hours and still Uncle Ned didn't show up. I was getting worried, and I kept suggesting new ideas for pictures, but I knew I couldn't hold out forever. Finally at around three, Woody said to the photographer, "What do you think?" and he said, "I guess I've got enough."

"Gee, we hardly took any pictures of me inside the house. I would think the magazine would want a lot of shots of me making the beds and vacuum-cleaning the living room."

Woody looked at me. "You're supposed to be The Boy Next Door, not Cinderella," he said. "Let's get out of this hick town."

The photographer began packing his stuff and we started to get into the car. Then at the last minute a kid ran up with a pencil and a piece of paper and asked for my autograph. I gave it to him and that started everybody getting pieces of paper and borrowing pens from each other and asking for my autograph—except the kids my own age, who stood around sneering and making sorehead remarks. I signed my name as slowly as I could, but finally there was nobody left.

"Come on, George," Woody said.

So we climbed into the Rolls and took off. All the way through town I kept leaning out of the window hoping that Uncle Ned would come along and see me, and send the cops after me. But he didn't and then we were out on the highway, heading for New York.

All the way down my heart kept sinking lower and lower, because I knew that sooner or later Superman was going to call me in and ask me if I'd delivered the tapes all right. It really scared me.

We got back to the city around five o'clock.

The P.R. guys left Woody and me at the Camelot Building, and then took the car back to the rental place. "Come up and let's have a look at tomorrow's schedule," Woody said. So we went up and into the reception room of Superman's office where his secretary sat. "Is his majesty in?" Woody asked.

"He's in, but he's busy," she said.

"What's on for tomorrow?"

She picked up a piece of paper and looked it over. "Nothing special. George is supposed to work with Damon Damon."

Woody slapped me on the back. "Got that, kid?"

"Okay," I said. We turned and started to go. Then the secretary said, "George, Superman told me to ask you to stick around for a while. He said he wanted to talk to you about something. He said it was important."

CHAPTER THIRTEEN

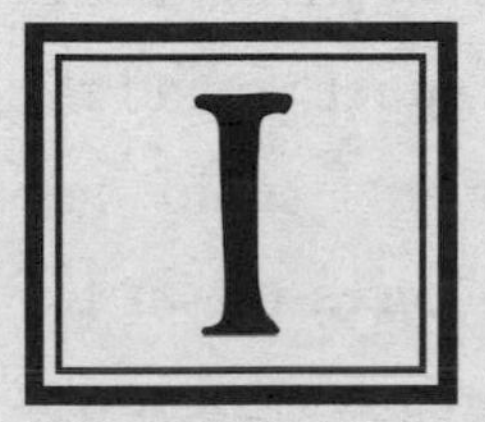

SAT THERE IN the reception room reading *Rolling Stone* and trying to look bored and restless as if I hadn't a thing on my mind. It got to be six o'clock and then six-thirty, and then quarter to seven. Finally, I said to Superman's secretary, "Maybe he's too busy to see me. Maybe I should go home and see him tomorrow."

"He said he wanted to see you. You'd better stick around."

So I went on sitting. It got to be seven, and then quarter after, and then suddenly the door to Superman's office opened and he stuck his head out. "Be with you in a minute, George," he said. Then he said to the secretary, "You can go on home, Arlene. I'm just going to talk to George for five minutes, and then cut out myself." He shut the door. The secretary got up, put some stuff in her purse, dithered around for a few minutes, and left. I went on sitting there. It was beginning to get kind of quiet around the Camelot offices. In the distance, I could hear doors slamming and people's voices off in the distance by the elevators. The voices got fewer and fewer, with long gaps of silence in between. Finally, the only noise I could hear was the hum of the air conditioner in the reception room.

It made me nervous to be there all alone. I reached in my pocket and took out my teddy bear key chain. It made me feel better to have it around. I sort of rested it on my knee where I could look at it when I wanted to, and went on reading *Rolling Stone*. It got to be seven-thirty and then quarter to eight. And finally Superman's door opened again and there he was. "Come on in, George. Sorry I've been so long.

I'll only take a couple of minutes."

I got up. My knees were weak and my eyes felt sort of blurred. I walked into this room. He shut the door behind me and then he crutched himself over to his desk and sat down. I leaned against one of the chairs in front of his desk. I didn't feel like sitting down. I sort of had the idea of being able to run if I had to.

"Sit down," he said.

"It's okay," I said. "I don't mind standing."

"Sit down," he said. I sat down. He leaned back, his hands behind his head so that I could see those huge shoulder muscles swelling up, and stared at me out of those blue egg-eyes. "How did the shooting go up in Pawling?"

"Fine," I said. "I mean, I think it did. The photographer said it was okay."

"Glad to hear it. Now, what about those tapes I gave you last night—did they get delivered all right?"

I could feel myself go hot and the sweat start to drip down my side under my shirt. "I guess so," I said. "The guy wasn't there, but I left them outside his door. I figured nobody would steal a box of tapes."

"You sure you left them there, George?"

I scratched my head. "Sure I am," I said.

"You sure you didn't take them home with you?"

That scared me. "No, honest, Superman."

He took his hands down from behind his head and leaned forward, staring into my face. "It surprises me to hear you say that, Boy Next Door," he said in a kind of soft, scary voice, "because when I picked the lock on your old man's door last night and broke into your apartment, I found the tapes on the dining table."

I sat bolt still, I couldn't move my mouth to answer, I couldn't even think.

"And the reason why I happened to do that, Boy Next Door, was because not long after you left my place with those boxes, the guy you were supposed to deliver them to got busted."

"I didn't know that," I sort of whispered.

"Nobody answered the door so I figured I'd better take them home."

"And then what happened, Boy Next Door?"

"Nothing," I whispered. "We went out to the movies and when we came back the package was gone."

"Too many coincidences there." He shook his head. "Nope, Boy Next Door. You got to look at it my way. I give you some boxes to deliver and fifteen minutes later the guy you're supposed to deliver them to gets busted. Kind of funny, isn't it? And what I want to know is what you did right after you left my apartment."

"Honest, Superman, I didn't do anything, I just went to the address."

"Oh, come on, Boy Next Door."

"I swear I didn't do anything," I blurted out. "I didn't even know there was cocaine in them until—" I stopped, because I knew I'd maybe got myself killed with this mistake.

He sat there at his desk staring at me with his big egg-eyes. He didn't say anything for a long time, he just stared at me. And then he said in that soft voice, "How did you *know* what was in those boxes?"

"I wanted to listen to my tapes," I whispered. I felt cold and frozen, so I couldn't move.

He stared at me some more. Then he said, "Nope, Boy Next Door. About three minutes after you left my place you called the police and gave them the address from the package, and they went down there and busted that guy. Now I want to know the whole story. And if I don't get it, Boy Next Door, it will not be well with you."

I just stared at him. What could I say? It didn't much matter anymore whether he believed me. Now he knew that I had seen the cocaine. The one thing about Superman was that he couldn't run: if you could get away from him he couldn't catch you. And the thing was, could I leap out of the chair and make a dash for the door? Why not? Of course he might have a gun in his desk—there was no way of knowing. A big executive like Superman would always have some excuse for having a gun; that he had to carry around a lot of money all the time or that people were always trying to steal his recording secrets. So there was a danger in that. But then I remembered that Superman had been in jail. It seemed to me that somebody who had been in jail wasn't allowed to get a gun permit. Of course, to somebody like Superman, having a gun permit wouldn't matter very much, if he decided to get one. But still, it seemed to me worth the chance to make a dash for the door.

"Come on, Boy Next Door. Let's have it."

"It's the truth," I said. Feeling so frozen and scared the way I was, I wasn't sure that I could even get moving. I began to count to three to myself. He leaned back in his chair. I got to three. I just stood up and swiveled out of the chair and raced for the door. It seemed to be miles away, like in one of those dreams when you keep running and running and can't seem to get anywhere. Then I was there, lunging for the door handle. I twisted it. It didn't turn. The door was locked.

"Turn around, Boy Next Door."

I turned around. Superman was still sitting at his desk, but he was holding out in front of him a metal contraption that at first I didn't recognize. Then I saw what it was—one of his crutches. Except that something was different about it. The rubber tip was gone from the end; instead, there was a sharp point, sharp as a spear.

"Interesting-looking thing, isn't it, Boy Next Door," he said. He turned it a bit sideways, so I could see it better. "You see how it works? That leg part of the crutch looks solid, but it isn't. Inside of it there's a spring and this lovely-looking piece of aluminum rod with a nice, sharp point on it. All I have to do is touch this tiny lever here to release the spring, and zing—out shoots the rod at a pretty good clip."

He patted it admiringly. "My own invention. Oh, I don't want to make too much out of it. It isn't terribly accurate beyond fifty feet. But usually that's close enough."

I just stared at him. I remembered about the man Damon had told me about, who'd got murdered the time Superman had got busted. He'd been killed with some sort of spear thing, Damon had said.

"All right, Boy Next Door. Come and sit down again. We haven't finished talking."

I went back to the chair and sat down again. Slowly he pushed the spear gun crutch across the desk, until the point of it was touching my shirt.

"I didn't do anything, Superman." I reached my hand in my pocket to feel for my teddy bear key chain. It wasn't there. I tried the other pocket—and then I remembered that it had been sitting on my knee when Superman had come into the reception room. It must have fallen onto the floor when I stood up. That made me feel more scared. I wished I had it.

"Boy Next Door," he said softly, "if you so much as wiggle I'll run this through you."

I nodded again. I was too scared even to talk.

"Okay, Boy Next Door. It's truth and consequences time."

I nodded again. I still couldn't speak. I just sat there, stiff and rigid.

"I'm going to ask a few questions," he said. "And if I don't get the truth, you get the consequences. Each time I don't like your answer I'm going to make a little hole in you. And if I were you, Boy Next Door, I'd be careful how I answered, because if you get too many little holes in you, the blood will all leak out. Understand?"

I nodded.

"Answer."

"I understand," I whispered.

"Okay, Boy Next Door. How'd you find out I was dealing coke?"

I couldn't speak. I was too scared.

He gave the spear gun a little push, so that the point pricked my skin.

"I didn't know. Honest."

"Come off it, Boy Next Door."

"Honest, Superman," I whispered. "I didn't know anything about it. I didn't tell the cops."

"Ha,ha,ha," he said.

"Please, Superman, I didn't know anything. I just wanted to hear my tapes."

"That's why you took them home?"

"No, I took them down to where the address said. I really did. I rang the bell six times, but nobody answered."

He grunted.

"It's true."

"Nobody answered the bell, that much I know is true," he said, "because he was on his way to the station house." He sat and thought about it for a minute. "But I don't get the rest of it. How did you know I was dealing?"

"I didn't know," I croaked.

"Cut the crap," he snarled. He gave the crutch an other little shove, pricking my skin again, but a little deeper this time. "Truth or consequences, Boy Next Door."

I wondered if anybody would hear me if I screamed. The sound would have to go through two doors and down a hall. Being a record company, everything was pretty soundproof. Suppose I screamed, what could Superman do? Would he kill me right then and there? What would happen if somebody came? If I went on screaming, Superman would probably bash me on the head. There was a window open, though. I wondered if anybody down on the street would hear me if I screamed. Maybe if there were some windows open on the floor below somebody might hear me. I wondered if I could get to the open window.

"Boy Next Door," Superman said softly, "I want to *know* what the police know." He gave another push on the spear, and I wriggled.

"Superman, it's the honest truth, I swear. I

never called the police. I was going to, but I never did, and then when the cocaine was gone I decided not to. The police wouldn't believe me, anyway."

He stared at me for a minute. "Boy Next Door, you almost convince me. But not quite. How the hell did the police happen to bust that guy so quick after you got the package with his address on it?"

The sweat was pouring down my face. "It must have been a coincidence. I swear I didn't tell anybody anything."

He went on staring at me. I knew he wouldn't want to kill me until he found out what the police knew. The thing was if I could only get the spear away from him.

"It's a hell of a funny coincidence," he said.

If I could suddenly swivel sideways somehow, I figured I could grab the crutch spear gun and push it to one side. If I jerked probably it would go off, and then I could grab the spear before Superman got it. "It's the truth," I said.

He didn't know whether to believe me or not. He leaned back his chair, and pulled the spear gun back so that it was a foot away from my chest. He held it sort of loosely, and went on staring at me. He wasn't in a hurry about anything. He was taking his time. "You know, I almost believe you. The one part I can't figure out is how you could have found out about the coke." He was almost talking to himself. "The only way that it makes any sense is if somebody around here got suspicious and went to the cops. But why bring you into it, Boy Next Door? What did they need to involve a kid for? It doesn't make sense."

"I swear, Superman, it was just a coincidence."

He stared at me, and then he sort of rubbed his chin and looked up at the ceiling. I took a deep breath. Then I leaped out of the chair. His free hand shot back to the spear gun. I grabbed the end and pushed it away from me. At the same moment he pulled the trigger. There was a kind of whooshing noise. I felt my side burn. Then there was a kind of heavy smacking sound as the spear slammed into the door and stuck, quivering rapidly back and forth. "I'll get you yet," Superman shouted. He began to heave himself up out of his chair. I turned, raced for the door, and grabbed onto the spear. It was pretty stuck. I gave it a good jerk. The point squeaked in the wood. I jerked it again and it came loose. Then I swung around.

Superman was hobbling across the floor on his crutches. The spear gun one was about six inches shorter than the other one, and it made it hard for him to move along. He was heading right for me. I let him get up to about five feet from me, then I skipped off to one side and raced back across the room. As long as I could keep away from him I was okay, but if he managed to get the spear back, I was in trouble. He turned and stood staring at me. Then he began to move forward again, this time going slowly, a step at a time, and watching me like a cat watching a bird, his big egg-eyes fastened on me like clamps. He was going to try to close in on me slowly, and corner me somewhere. I figured he'd probably try to hit me with one of his crutches if he could. With arms as strong as his, he'd be able to hurt me pretty bad if he hit me. I stood there, watching. Slowly he closed in. I felt a little breeze behind me, blowing in through the window. It reminded me that it was open. I turned and shouted out, "Help, he's trying to kill me." Little car noises floated up from below—faint horn honkings and the sound of a bus starting up from the curb. The sun was gone and it was night, but down in the cavern between the buildings there was a kind of sea of light, which got fainter as it came up. It was a long way down. I turned toward Superman. He was closing in, about ten feet away. I was still holding the spear in my hands. I stuck it out in front of me toward him. He started to grab for it, and quickly I realized that was a mistake and I jerked it back. With those strong arms he could easily pull it out of my hands once he got hold of the end. And the minute he had the spear back I was done for. I pressed back against the window. He hitched forward on his crutches. Now he was only five feet away. There was no place for me to go, except out the window. I turned to face it. What I wanted to do was fling the spear out the window, but I didn't dare, because it would probably kill somebody down on the street below. At that height it would be going like a rocket by the time it hit the ground.

I turned back. Superman was closer. He raised up one crutch, sort of balancing himself on the other, and started to swing it around. I jumped up on the windowsill. Then I swung out the window and around the edge so I was standing on the ledge, with my face pressed up against the side of the Camelot Building, with the spear still in my hand. The only thing I had to hold on to was the edge of the window. I looked down. I could see the street straight down below me, just past my shoes—all those yellow taxis and buses and cars going up and down the streets in that hazy light. I began to feel dizzy and trembly, and I stopped looking down.

Superman was standing by the window, looking up at me and grinning. "Where are you going to now, Boy Next Door? It couldn't have worked out better, could it? All I do is reach out the window, give your leg a pull, and down you go. I'll tell the newspapers that it was a tragic accident—so talented a boy to die by accidentally falling out a window." He reached for my leg. I kicked at his hand and he pulled it back. Then he reached again. I kicked, but he caught it and held it. I tried to jerk loose, but I couldn't kick around too much without losing my balance. He started to twist my foot around. I could feel my whole body being forced to turn away from the window and out toward the street.

And then suddenly he stopped and turned

away from the window. "Who is it?" he shouted. "Go away, I'm busy." There was a kind of heavy bumping noise, and then another, and then a splintering crash of wood. "What the hell is this?" Superman shouted. I slipped in from the window, and sat on the windowsill, my legs dangling into the room. There was another splintering crash, and the door broke and swung inward, and all of a sudden the room was full of cops, swarming all over the place. Behind them was Woody, and behind him was Barbara Feinberg. I slipped off the windowsill, my legs and arms trembling so much I could hardly stand up, and then Woody and Barbara were sort of holding me up. About two minutes later the cops had got handcuffs on Superman and were leading him out of the room; and then Barbara was giving me a can of soda she'd got from the machine in the hall, and the cops were asking me a million questions, most of which I didn't know the answers to. And then finally we went downstairs to the bottom floor, and there was the television news crew with their cameras, and the story all came out.

When I hadn't come home, Barbara had got worried. She'd found Woody's phone number in my address book and called him, and of course he said that we'd all got back from the shooting in Pawling hours before. That worried her even more, and so she spilled it all to Woody about the cocaine. And suddenly Woody remembered that Superman had asked me to see him; and that was when everything began to add up, and he and Barbara came up to Camelot looking for me.

"The crazy thing is," Barbara said, "we came up here practically an hour ago. The door was locked and we figured whatever had happened, Superman had left. We started to leave, and then I saw your teddy bear key chain lying on the floor in the reception room. That was when we figured you were in there, and we called the cops."

So I told my story on television, not trying

to make myself out a hero or anything, but as usual they got it wrong, and it came out in the news that I'd discovered Superman was dealing in coke, and I tracked him down in his lair. I was trying to explain that I didn't track Superman down, when Woody Woodward burst in and said, "This is no ordinary kid, he's one of the country's most talented young vocal stars, he's hot as a jet of live steam."

"He's what?" one of the reporters asked.

"He's just signed a Camelot recording contract. He's moving like a fire engine."

And that's the way it came out on the television and in the newspapers—"Young Singer Outwits Dope Mobster." I felt sort of guilty about everybody thinking I had outsmarted Superman, but I'll admit it, not guilty enough to say anything about it. When the kids asked me about it later, I just said, "Oh well, it sort of happened."

Finally they let us go, and Woody and Barbara and I rode down to our apartment in a taxicab. It was about midnight. "Oh boy, George," Woody said.

"Why was it my fault, Woody?"

"Whosever fault," he said, "The Boy Next Door is down the drain."

Frankly, I was just as glad. "Woody, how come it was my fault that Superman tried to kill me?"

"I don't know, George. It just seems that every time something gets hot, you get into one of these crazy things."

"Well, it wasn't my fault."

He sighed. "I guess not." He was quiet for a minute. We were passing through Times Square and I looked out the window at the lights and the people hustling and bustling around. Then Woody said, "Well, let's look on the bright side. Maybe the publicity will help. Maybe I can think of something."

"What's worrying me is, what am I going to tell Pop?"

"Tell Pop? Doesn't he know about this?"